D1153015

60000252212

Sch

A Boy and a Bear in a Boat

www.**davidficklingbooks**.co.uk

Also by Dave Shelton

Good Dog, Bad Dog

A Boy
and a Bear
in a Boat

Dave Shelton

David Fickling Books

A BOY AND A BEAR IN A BOAT
A DAVID FICKLING BOOK 978 0 385 61896 0
Published in Great Britain by David Fickling Books,
a division of Random House Children's Books
A Random House Group Company

This edition published 2012

All ri   l in

a re   c,

mechai **Northamptonshire** ssion

LRE

The Rand   FSC®), the

leading inte   C label are

printed on   idorsed by

the leading   ocurement

Askews & Holts

Set in 13/19pt New Baskerville by Falcon Oast Graphic Art.

DAVID FICKLING BOOKS
31 Beaumont Street, Oxford, OX1 2NP

www.kidsatrandomhouse.co.uk
www.totallyrandombooks.co.uk
www.randomhouse.co.uk

Addresses for companies within The Random House Group Limited can be found
at: www.randomhouse.co.uk/offices.htm

THE RANDOM HOUSE GROUP Limited Reg. No. 954009

A CIP catalogue record for this book is available from the British Library.

Printed and bound in China.

For Pam

Stepping Aboard

"Welcome aboard," said the bear, standing and turning to face the boy. He had been holding the boat steady as the boy got in. Now he released his grip on the wooden jetty and pushed them out into the water and the boy felt an unsteadiness beneath his feet.

"Hello," said the boy. The rolling of the boat put a tremble in his voice.

"Where to?" said the bear.

The boy wobbled back to the rear

seat, concentrating as the hull rolled and bounced beneath him. He half sat and half fell onto the hard wooden bench, bashing his wrist painfully against the edge as he landed.

"Ow!" he said. "Just over to the other side, please." He waved his unbashed hand vaguely out across the water without looking up.

"Right you are," said the bear.

The boy stowed his
bag beneath his seat.
He found a gap
in the jumble
of junk already
taking up most of
the space there
and then pushed
quite hard to

persuade the bag into place. There was a
small crunching noise. The boy looked up
guiltily towards the bear, but it seemed he
hadn't heard. He was sitting on the front
seat fitting the oars into place. He dipped
the blade of one oar into the water and
pulled on it briefly, turning the boat to face
away from the jetty. The boy felt the boat
wobble and then settle, and the insides of
his stomach did the same. The bear took
a look over his shoulder and squinted

into the distance. He made a small low noise. Then he reached forward, dropped the blades of the oars into the water and pulled back on the handles in a long, easy movement, setting the boat into motion.

"Away we go," he said.

"Will it take long?" said the boy.

"A little while," said the bear.

Away from the shade of the jetty they were in the full glare of the sun and the boy felt itchily hot. He took off his coat and scrunched it up on the seat beside him. He looked at the bear. He was a big bear and the boat was only a small boat. When he leaned forward at the start of each stroke it was as if he were lunging towards the boy, reaching out to grab at him. And the boat pitched and rolled and bounced as if the world had become unfixed. It was a little unnerving. He would be glad to get where he was going, back on firm ground again. He looked past the bear, out over the water ahead of them.

"You can't even see it from here, can you?" he said. "I thought you'd be able to see it."

"No, it's quite a way," said the bear.

The boy leaned back and raised his face towards the sun. He closed his eyes and played with the colours of darkness he could see by pressing his eyelids more or less tightly together. He liked the greeny blue the best, but it was difficult to hold on to for long. He yawned and lolled his head forward and his eyes fell open again.

He watched the bear. It was a reassuring sight. He rowed as if it were the most natural movement he could make. As natural as walking, or breathing even. He had a steady, casual rhythm and seemed to be making almost no effort at all but the boat sped along just the same. The boy closed his eyes again and listened to the rhythm of the oars.

Splish, splish, splish . . .

It was rather calming. And the boat was only gently rocking now, soothing rather than unsettling him. He leaned out over the side of the boat and looked down at the water, watching through half-closed eyes the dancing patterns of sunlit ripples. Then he trailed a hand in the water and made patterns of his own. The water was cold, but pleasingly so. He pulled his hand back inside the boat and yawned again. Without realising it, he had pulled his legs up onto the seat so that he was lying on it, curled up to fit the space. The sunlight on the water was too bright for comfort so he moved his head back inside the boat, resting it on his bunched-up coat. He looked at the weave of the fabric, picked out in detail by the sunlight. He felt the warmth of the sun on his skin. He listened to the oars, steady as a heartbeat, and the gently lapping waves. He felt the sway of the boat beneath him, rocking like a cradle.

He closed his eyes.

Unforeseeable Anomalies

When the boy opened his eyes again he couldn't think for a moment where he was. But then the faint taste of salt on his lips, the smell of damp fur and the sound of oars dipping into water – *splish, splish, splish* – all helped remind him. And then his bleary eyes focused and he saw the bear.

Oh, yes.

He sat up, shrugging off a tatty blanket that had been draped over him, and

8

blinked hard twice. Then he looked past the bear. There was still no sign of land ahead of them. But there was no sign of the land they'd set out from behind them either. In fact in every direction all he could see was sea and sky.

He looked at his watch but it showed exactly the same time now as it had when they had set off. He held it to his ear but it was silent.

"It's stopped," he said, sleepily.

The bear looked at him, as if noticing him for the first time.

"Good morning,"
said the bear.

The boy stared at him with wide, awake eyes.

"What?" he said.

"Good morning,"

said the bear again, a little puzzled.

"Morning?" said the boy.

"Yes," said the bear.

"It's morning?" said the boy.

"Yes," said the bear.

"So . . . it's tomorrow?" said the boy.

The bear considered this.

"Well, no," he said. "Obviously it can't be tomorrow, can it? It's today. It's always today, isn't it? But, yes, it is the today that was tomorrow yesterday. If you see what I mean."

"So I slept all night?" said the boy. "I thought I'd just had a nap."

"Oh no," said the bear. "You were asleep for hours."

"But," said the boy, frowning, "doesn't that mean we should be there by now? I mean, I know you said it would take a little while, but I thought you meant an hour or

10

so, not all night. So shouldn't we be there? Or at least be able to see it by now?"

"Oh, I see what you mean," said the bear. "Well, yes, normally we would have arrived by now but unfortunately there were . . . unforeseeable anomalies in the currents and we had to adjust our course a bit. So now we're running a little behind schedule. Sorry."

"Oh, I see," said the boy. He didn't see at all. "But are we *nearly* there?"

"Not really, no."

The boy's face fell.

"But everything is in hand," said the bear. "Don't worry."

The bear stopped rowing, pulled in the oars and, with a little difficulty, took out from under his seat a large, battered suitcase. He opened it up and took out a folded-up piece of old, yellowed paper.

He rather clumsily unfolded it and then held it in front of him as if he were reading a large newspaper. The side that the boy could see was unmarked, except for a few smears of dirt and a squashed bug, but one corner had flopped over so that the boy could see just a little of what was printed on the other side. There was a corner of blue with a grid marked over it and numbers along the edges. So at least the bear had a

map. That was reassuring.

The bear examined the map closely. In fact, the boy could see, from his side, a bump in the paper where the bear's nose was pressed against it. The bump moved about a bit and the bear hummed and mumbled to himself. Then the bear folded up the map (which took him three attempts), put it back in the case and took out a telescope. He put it to his eye and

looked out across the sea ahead of them, and hummed and mumbled some more. Then he put the telescope away and, with a little more difficulty than it had taken to get it out, put the case back beneath his seat.

"Is everything all right?" said the boy.

The bear shook off a slight frown and turned a smile in the boy's direction.

"Oh yes," he said. "Absolutely tickity boo."

The boy assumed that "tickity boo" was a good thing.

"Just need to keep an eye on where we are. Don't want to run into any sea monsters, do we?" said the bear.

The boy was a bit alarmed by this until he realised that the bear was joking. At least, he was fairly sure he was joking, though he chose not to ask.

"And are we nearly there yet?" said the boy.

"We're well on our way," said the bear.

The boy shivered and picked up his coat.

"By the way," said the bear, "did you happen to bring any food with you?"

Breakfast

The boy hadn't been hungry before the bear had mentioned food but now he was ravenous. He freed his bag from beneath his seat and set about the food that he had brought with him. He ate both his sandwiches (cheese and pickle, one of each), one bag of crisps, a banana and three of his favourite fizzy blackcurrant sweets that turned his tongue purple. And he drank a bottle of ginger beer.

The bear ate too. He took out a large,

scratched and dented metal lunch box from under his seat and extracted from it one small triangular sandwich (with the crusts cut off) and ate it with great delicacy in many nibbled bites, savouring each one.

A strange smell wafted over to the boy.

"What was in that?" he said.

"Broccoli, sherbet and gooseberry," said the bear. "Delicious!"

"That's a good big lunch box you've got," said the boy.

"Oh yes," said the bear, contemplating its contents once again. "I'm not really a big eater, but I like to bring along plenty of sandwiches just in case."

"Just in case? In case of what?"

"Oh, you know," said the bear, daintily selecting another sandwich. "Emergencies."

"And," said the boy, as casually as he could, "do you have a lot of emergencies?"

"Oh, you know, a few," said the bear
brightly. "They keep life interesting, don't
they, emergencies?" He took a small bite
from the sandwich. "Mmm . . . anchovy,
banana and custard. Yum!"

When he had finished, he put the lunch

box away and set back to rowing, away from the nothing-at-all that lay behind them and on towards another lot of nothing-at-all ahead of them.

Splish, splish, splish . . .

It wasn't that the boy was worried exactly. He was sure that the bear knew what he was doing. Well, fairly sure anyway. He would just have been happier if he could have seen land. Or another boat. Or anything, really, that wasn't sea or sky. There weren't even any aeroplanes or birds or clouds to look at, which was a bit odd. And a bit boring.

Idly, the boy dunked his empty pop bottle into the sea and brought it up full of sea water. He turned it over, watching the thin torrent of falling water catching the light and listening to the glugs and splashes that it made. Then he did it again.

Twice was enough, it turned out. It wasn't that interesting.

He sighed and contemplated the bar of chocolate in his bag. He loved chocolate but, on balance, decided not to have any just now. He would save it for later. In case of emergencies.

The bear was singing to himself as he rowed now, in a sweet, high, quavering voice. It reminded the boy of his gran singing hymns in the kitchen while she did the washing-up. The bear sang so softly that the boy could make out neither the

words nor the tune, but it was clearly quite jolly, whatever it was, and that was rather reassuring. The bear certainly seemed to enjoy his work, grinning as he sang as he rowed. The boy decided not to disturb him with any of the questions he would like to ask. Instead, he took a look around. That didn't take long. Outside the boat was the same view in every direction. Inside the boat there wasn't space for very much that might be interesting to look at. The bear kept the bottom of the boat absolutely clear (he had even been careful to gather

up his sandwich crumbs and put them in an old treacle tin that he used as a bin) and anything that might be worth looking at was stored under the seats in a jumble of shadows. It was a mess, and rather a boring one, just old tins and packets and boaty things, and no toys at all (apart from, curiously, a small yellow plastic duck).

The boy stood up, rather unsteadily, and stretched his limbs. He would have liked a walk but had to settle for shuffling round in a tiny wobbly circle in the cramped space between the rear and middle seats. He shuffled and scuffed and wobbled, and then, frustrated and bored, sat back down and sighed quietly. Then, when the bear failed to notice, he sighed loudly.

The bear looked up.

"Are you . . . bored?" said the bear. He seemed rather puzzled by the idea.

"Well, yes, a bit," said the boy.

"Bored?" said the bear. "How can you be bored? I don't understand it. Out on the sea on a beautiful day in the best little dinghy in all the world – what could be better?"

"Arriving?" said the boy, but the bear took no notice.

"Bored, eh? Well, I suppose you'd better try the complimentary on-board entertainment then," said the bear.

"On-board entertainment?" said the boy, smiling expectantly.

"Oh yes," said the bear. "You'll love this."

On-Board Entertainment

It wasn't going well.

"I spy," said the bear, "with my little eye something beginning with . . . um, let me see . . ." He looked all around, frowning. Then he looked upwards and smiled. ". . . S," he said.

"Sky?" said the boy wearily.

The bear looked almost shocked. Then his grin returned, wider than ever.

"That's right," said the bear. "You know, you really are very good at this."

"Thanks," said the boy, without enthusiasm.

"Your turn," said the bear.

"I spy with my little—"

"Hoy, now, you've got to have your little eye open if you're going to spy anything."

Wearily slumped on the rear seat with his head in his hands,

the boy opened his eyes halfway, staring up from under furious eyebrows at the bear. He began again, his voice bored and flat.

26

"I spy with my little eye something beginning with S."

"Oh, I know," said the bear. "Hang on . . ." He furrowed his brow in concentration, rolled his eyes up to one side, down at the deck, up to the other side, scrunched them shut, opened them again, tapped his foot, scratched his head, scratched his bottom, scratched an ear, muttered to himself, waggled his jaw, hummed a little. The boy half

27

expected smoke to come out of his ears he seemed to be thinking so hard.

"Is it . . . oh, no, hang on . . . er . . . oh, I know, it's . . . um . . ."

All the eye rolling and scratching and tapping and waggling stopped for a moment and the bear looked blankly at the boy.

"Um, what did you say it began with again?" said the bear.

"S," said the boy. *Like everything we've spied for the last hour,* he thought.

28

"Oh yes. S. Hmm, that's a good one. Let's see now . . ."

Oh, for goodness' sake, thought the boy. He looked out of the boat at the rippling water. He stared at it hard. Then he stared at the bear. Then he stared at the water again. He fixed the bear's gaze and then nodded in the direction of the water. The bear looked at him blankly. Then, slowly, a smile arrived on his face, creeping over it like a reluctant dawn.

"Sky," said the bear.

"No."

"It's not sky?"

"No."

"Oh. I was so sure it was sky. And it definitely begins with S?"

"Yes."

The boy nodded at the water again. Trailed his hand in it. Splashed it about a bit.

The bear had an expression of mighty concentration again but clearly wasn't taking the hint. In desperation the boy began to sing, softly, under his breath.

"A sailor went to sea, sea, sea . . ." he whispered.

The bear looked around him, squinting and frowning.

"To see what he could see, see, see . . ." sang the boy.

The bear looked confused.

"But all that he could *see, see, see* . . ." sang the boy, jabbing a finger towards the water.

The bear closed his eyes and shook his head, as if trying to dislodge a thought that had got stuck somehow.

The boy sang louder.

"Was the bottom of the deep blue *sea, sea, sea.*"

He was almost shouting by the end, leaning forward and staring hard at the bear in exasperation, pointing at the water with one hand and miming a wave-like motion with the other.

"Sea?" said the bear uncertainly.

"Yes," said the boy, slumping where he sat as if exhausted. "Well done."

"Oh goody! My turn again," said the bear. "I spy with my little eye something beginning with S."

"Sky," said the boy.

"Crikey!" said the bear. "You really are *very* good at this, aren't you? Have you played a lot before?"

"A bit. Look, Bear, do you think, if we're going to play, that we could maybe change your rules a bit so we can spy things *inside* the boat as well as outside?"

"Ooh no, that would make it much too hard. Besides, I don't know how to spell most of the things in here. Come on. Your turn."

"But . . ."

"Come on, just a few more rounds. I really think I'm starting to get the hang of it now."

"But . . . Oh, OK."

The boy looked around, just in case, but all he saw was sea and sky.

"I spy . . ." he said.

He leaned over the side of the boat with his arms up on the edge and his chin resting on the backs of his hands.

". . . with my little eye . . ." he said.

His head slumped forward, as if he no longer had the energy to hold it up. He gazed down along the side of the boat to the water.

". . . something beginning . . ." he said.

There was something written on the side of the boat, painted neatly in delicate joined-up writing, clear enough to read even upside down.

". . . with H," he said, a note of surprise in his voice.

He looked at the bear. The bear was smiling.

"*Harriet*," said the bear.

The *Harriet*

"**W**hy is your boat called *Harriet?*" said the boy.

He wasn't really all that interested but at least it stopped them having to play I Spy any more.

The bear kept rowing and turned his head to look over his shoulder at the way they were going.

"I named her after . . . a friend of mine," said the bear out of the corner of his mouth.

"There's a Harriet in my class at school," said the boy. "Harriet Bailey."

"Oh yes," said the bear. "Is she nice?"

"No," said the boy. "Not really."

"Oh," said the bear.

"At least not so nice that you'd name a boat after her."

"Oh," said the bear.

"What's your Harriet like then?" said the boy.

"Well, I don't really know any more. I haven't seen her for a while." The bear stopped rowing to scratch his nose. "But she used to be all the things that I hoped the boat would be."

"Like what?" said the boy.

"Well," said the bear, "she was very strong and very reliable . . ."

He was looking up and away now, into the distance and the past, and smiling.

". . . and very buoyant," he said. Then he grinned broadly, directly at the boy, and pulled on the oars once more. Then he started singing again, a little more loudly than before.

The boy took a new look around the boat. His first thought was that it wasn't much of a compliment to have a battered little boat like this named after you. But

on closer inspection he changed his mind. She was an old boat, clearly, but well looked-after. Loved, even. Although the waters had washed and worn her timbers over many years, it was clear that they had been freshly painted, and with considerable care. And the metal fittings gleamed, even if some of them were held in place by as many as three different sizes of screw. There were signs of any number of repairs if you looked for them, but you really did have to look for them. They had been carried out with such patience and care that they were barely visible. It would be impressive work from a skilled carpenter, let alone from a bear who could barely fold a map.

"She sounds very nice," said the boy, but the bear showed no sign of having heard him, he just kept smiling and rowing.

The Comic

Lunchtime came and went, but there wasn't much lunch involved.

The boy watched the horizon and waited for land to appear. It didn't. Then he closed his eyes and counted to a hundred as slowly as he could, then opened them again. Still no sign. Then he closed his eyes, started to count to two hundred, got bored at 124, and opened them again. Still nothing.

He reached under his seat for the

chocolate, but when he tugged at his bag it didn't move. He tugged harder, but still it wouldn't budge so he got off the seat and crouched down to take a closer look. Some sort of booklet had got caught and crumpled up between the bag and the side of the boat and jammed it into place. He took hold of the bag with one hand and pulled it sideways to make a little space, then worked the booklet free with the other hand. It was a comic. Brilliant! The boy loved comics. It wasn't one that he recognised and it was very badly creased but that didn't matter. He laid it on the seat and did his best to flatten it out. Then he read it.

Only he couldn't.

"What language is this?" he said, flapping it about in frustration.

He had only meant to say it to himself,

but the bear looked up at him.

"Oh that," said the bear. "I'm not sure. Get all sorts on board in my line of work, but never been any good with languages. Nice young fella though, the chap that left it behind."

The bear looked up and sideways, remembering.

"Nervous type but very pleasant. Big tipper too. Very generous. Or else he didn't really understand our money properly, I'm not sure." Then he shook out the thoughtful crumples in his forehead, smiled broadly and began to sing again, back in his own happy world of rowing and paying the boy no attention at all.

The boy flicked quickly through the comic, hoping that he might be able to make out some of the story from the pictures alone, but it was no good. It

seemed to be just one episode of a longer
story so it didn't have a proper beginning
or ending, it was all just part of the middle.
There was no way of knowing what had
gone on before or what would happen
after. And, actually, the boy didn't have
much of a clue about what was going on
now.

It wasn't just that he didn't understand the words (although he did notice that "Aaargh!" was spelled the same way), the pictures seemed foreign to him too. The drawings were weird, all angular and ugly and a little bit scary, and the colours didn't fit inside the lines.

He didn't like it at all. But he went through it a second time just the same (after all, he had nothing better to do). It still didn't make much sense, but he did find a couple of bits quite exciting.

Early on, a young girl (who seemed to be the heroine) escaped from the clutches of an evil villain with a scary hairdo and a big black coat. On the last page she was facing seemingly certain death at the claws of a gigantic slimy monster with a million teeth and, so far as the boy could make out, supernaturally bad breath. Most of what came in between, though, remained a mystery to him.

He gave up on it. It was stupid. But he was careful not to get it creased again when he put it away next to his bag.

Teatime

The boy was doing nothing very much, and had been for quite some time. He thought perhaps now he would do nothing at all for a while, just for a change.

The bear had rowed for all that time and so, presumably, they had travelled quite a long way, even though you wouldn't know it from the view. The boy had spent a long time gazing at the sea. He had counted waves for a while but lost interest after the first four hundred or so. He was roused from his bored daze by the bear suddenly freezing, mid-stroke. His oars hung motionless above the water, a strange wide-eyed expression on his face as if something had just struck him.

"What is it?" said the boy.

"It's four o'clock!" said the bear.

The boy had no way of knowing any different.

"And . . . ?" he said.

"Time for tea," said the bear.

He stopped rowing and pulled the oars part-way into the boat. Then he stood, turned, leaned down and pulled out his suitcase, and placed it on the middle seat. With dainty precision he removed from the case a small gas stove, a box of matches, a small battered and blackened kettle, a china teapot and a cup and saucer. Then he filled the kettle with water from a large plastic bottle. Then he lit the stove.

This was no simple matter as the bear appeared to be, quite simply, afraid of fire. First he opened the box of matches. Then he took out a match. Then he closed the box of matches. Then he put the matchbox down, with the match on top of it, next to the stove on the seat. Then, his face screwed up in concentration, he held the blue canister of the stove steady with one paw (at arm's length) while he grasped the knob to turn the gas on with the other. He was panting, just a little, the boy noticed. And very slightly quivering.

Then he turned the knob the tiniest fraction of a turn, grabbed quickly for the match and the matchbox, struck the match and held the flame to the burner, his face turned away and his free paw shielding his face.

Pft. The gas ignited pathetically into the tiniest blue flame. The bear let out a deep breath. Then he placed the kettle on the stove and turned up the gas so that the flame grew with a small roar. There was a whistle shaped like a bird at the end of the kettle's spout that sang shrilly when the water boiled, but not for long as the bear was watching closely and quickly turned the gas off. He used a little of the water to warm the teapot, swilling it around and then discarding it into the sea. Then he heaped in three teaspoons of leaf tea from a scratched and rusty tin, filled the pot from the kettle, replaced the lid and lovingly clad the pot in a pink woolly tea cosy with a pom-pom on the top. Then he reached beneath the seat and brought out a strangely-shaped black case. He opened it up and took out something that looked at once familiar and odd to the boy.

"What's wrong with your guitar?" said the boy. "Did it get wet and shrink?"

The bear gave him a stern look.

"It's not a guitar," he said. "It's a ukulele. I time my tea with a song." He plucked at the strings and adjusted the tuning. Then he began to play and sing.

When you are all at sea
You'll have a friend in me
We'll have a cup of tea
And keep on go-o-o-ing

The weather may be poor
With rain and wind and more
What fun! We just adore
It when it's sno-o-o-wing

You fear that you'll be drowned
The shark fins circle round
So what? We're homeward-bound
And we're not slo-o-o-wing

And if the current's strong
And the dark, cold night is long
Who cares? We'll sing our song
And just keep ro-o-o-wing

Mostly the bear strummed a very simple accompaniment to his singing, but between the final two verses he played quite a long complicated instrumental section. This wasn't something that he found easy judging by the faces that he pulled. He was obviously concentrating very hard. And the boy had to concentrate quite hard not to laugh.

When it was over, the bear put the ukulele away, removed the tea cosy and poured tea into his tea cup.

"Would you like some?" he said to the boy.

"No thanks," said the boy. He had never been able to see the point of tea. Even if you added loads of sugar, it was still boring.

Then the bear lifted the delicate china cup to his mouth, blew gently over the surface of its steaming contents and took a tiny sip.

"*Aaaaaaaaaaaaaaaaaaaaaaaaaaaaaaaah!*" sighed the bear.

And he smiled and stared into space, wearing an expression of deep contentment that he retained for the next quarter of an hour as he consumed, one small (and loudly appreciated) sip at a time, the rest of the contents of the cup. When he was done, he used the last drop of water from the kettle to rinse out his cup, emptied out the teapot into the sea, put everything neatly away and took up his oars again, beaming with happiness.

The boy watched him and tried a smile himself. He just about managed it but it was a bit of an effort.

Trust

Even by the end of the day, as he huddled under the blanket in the space between the rear and middle seats, the boy felt no doubt in the bear's abilities. The bear had explained that there had been "further complications" (though, out of kindness, he did not burden the boy with the details), and so there was a "regrettable additional delay" to their journey. But his jolly, confident manner was genuinely reassuring, and it was a mild night, and they would surely arrive early next morning.

The boy was sure that the bear knew what he was doing.

But by the end of the next day he was beginning to have doubts.

And by the afternoon of the day after that he was starting to get really quite worried.

The Maps

The boy was reading the comic again, as he had done the day before and the day before that. He still couldn't work out what was going on. He'd read it over and over, and the same things happened again and again, and none of it made any sense. A bit like the last three days, really. He gave up (again) and put the comic away under the seat.

Splish, splish, splish . . .

"Bear . . . ?"

The bear carried on rowing and looked at the boy grumpily.

"Don't you dare," he said, "say 'Are we nearly there yet?'"

"Oh. OK."

The bear said nothing more but made a point of huffing and puffing effortfully, despite rowing at the same even pace as ever, pushing the boat along at impressive speed without undue strain.

The boy stared out to sea and up into the sky, slowly taking in the view in all directions. He found nothing there to surprise him. He looked around the bottom of the boat, tidy as ever except for a bottle at the boy's feet containing the last couple of mouthfuls of ginger beer.

"Do you want some pop?"

The bear looked up, with a more kindly

air this time. "No. Thank you. There's not much left, is there? I think we'd better try to make it last. But you have it if you like."

"No. It's OK. I'll wait a bit."

Splish, splish, splish . . .

"Bear . . . ?"

"Yes."

"We will . . ." The boy hesitated, trying out the question in his head a few times. He wasn't sure it would go down too well.

"What?" said the bear, not too impatiently. Maybe it would be OK.

"We will be all right, won't we? I mean . . . we won't run out before we get there?"

"Of course not. Don't worry. We just need to be a little bit sensible with the supplies. Careful. Just to be on the safe side."

"Sensible," said the boy. "Yes, of course. And we're not . . ." Again he hesitated.

"What?" said the bear, evenly. He still seemed calm.

"We're not . . . now, don't take offence but, um . . ."

"What?"

"We're not lost, are we?"

The bear stopped rowing. For as long as it took for the boat to drift to a stop, he didn't say a word. Then he carried on not saying a word. And then after that he was silent for a while. And all this time he stared the boy straight in the eye.

"How dare you?" he said at last, slowly and quietly. "What do you take me for, some kind of incompetent?"

"No. Oh no. Not at all. It's just . . ."

"Well?"

"Well, it's been a long while, hasn't it? Even with anemones in the currents."

"Anomalies," said the bear.

"Anomalies, yes," said the boy.

"Yes," said the bear, his head still held in a defiant pose. "Anomalies in the currents. Yes. Tricky things, currents, you know. Nothing I could do. But everything's under control."

"So, we're not lost then?"

"No!"

The bear sounded defiant and angry,

but somehow he didn't look it. Something in his expression was wrong, unsure, unconvincing. He was almost looking at the boy, but not quite. The boy saw it at once. He rose from his seat and stared into the bear's eyes. The bear stared back. They stared at each other. For a long time.

The bear blinked first.

That clinched it.

"We are, aren't we? We're lost!" said the boy.

He felt triumphant as he said it, but not for long. A bear, after all, can't be expected to remain sheepish for long.

The bear growled as he stood. It was the first time the boy had heard him growl. It wasn't a loud growl, but somehow that just made it scarier. The *Harriet* rocked as the bear stepped towards the boy, shading him from the sun. The boy's confidence deserted him along with the light, and his stomach lurched. He was a small boy in a small boat with an angry bear. This did not seem ideal.

"WE . . ." said the bear.

The boy wondered about jumping overboard and swimming for it. He was quite a good swimmer.

". . . ARE . . ." shouted the bear.

The water looked really quite inviting. It wouldn't be that cold anyway. And so far as he knew there were no sharks about.

". . . NOT . . ." bellowed the bear.

The boy wondered if he had time to take his shoes and socks off first.

". . . *LOST!*" roared the bear.

The boy fell backwards onto his seat as if blown by a mighty wind.

"We are not lost!" repeated the bear, "I know exactly where we are. EXACTLY!

Here, see this?" He pulled a battered peaked white cap from his suitcase. It had an anchor emblem on the front. "Do you know what this is? Eh?" With a flourish he plonked the hat, somewhat askew, onto his head. "This is a captain's hat. I am the captain of this vessel and a captain, let me tell you, does not get lost. Are you satisfied now? Are you reassured? No? All right then. Let me show you, since you so plainly can't find it in yourself to trust the wisdom and experience of a bear who's been at sea all his life, since the instinct and intuition of your captain apparently aren't enough, then let me show you."

The bear opened up his suitcase again and took out the map.

"Let me show you," he said, "exactly where we are . . ." and he unfolded the map and laid it across the centre seat for

the boy to see.

"Here," he said, "precisely here. Here is where we are."

And he pointed. And the boy looked.

The map was perfectly square and entirely blue. All of it. There was no land, not even the tiniest island, marked anywhere. At first the boy thought that, down near the bottom left corner, there was a strange circular coral reef, but on closer inspection this proved to be a tea stain from the bottom of the bear's cup. The map depicted, in its entirety, flat, blue, featureless sea. He gawped at it, imagining the blue map as the actual sea, imagined himself looking down upon it from up in the air, imagined the *Harriet*, tiny and insignificant, at the spot close to the centre that the bear was pointing to.

"We really are in the middle of nowhere, aren't we?" said the boy.

The bear looked up at him, his anger dissipating as he saw the boy's deflated expression and the defeated slump of his shoulders.

"Oh no," he said. "Not the middle of

nowhere. No, not at all."

The boy raised his eyes to meet the bear's. Eager for any shred of comfort, but wary of false hope too.

"Really?" he said, suspiciously.

"Really," said the bear. He pointed again to the spot on the map he had indicated a moment earlier. "You see, we're here."

The boy stared at a small piece of the blue on the big blue map.

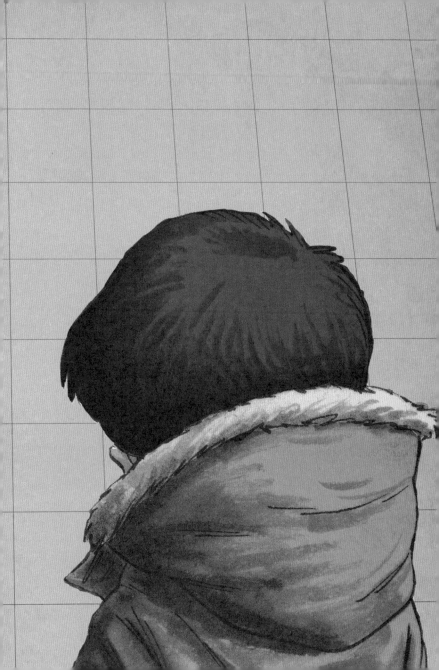

"And the *middle* of nowhere is here." The bear shifted his finger an inch or two down and to the right, and tapped the spot a couple of times for emphasis. "We passed through it at about noon yesterday. So you see it's not so bad."

The boy did not seem especially cheered by this. The bear shook off his bemusement and carried eagerly on.

"And, anyway, soon we'll be off that map and onto this one," he said, and proceeded to unfold a second map and place it flat over the top of the first. The boy stared at it. It was, again, very blue. His voice was cracking as he said, "There's nothing there. Just sea and sea and more sea. What's the point of even having a map with nothing but sea on it anyway?"

"I happen to like sea," said the bear indignantly. "And, in any case, this map is not just sea. Look here."

He pointed confidently to a biscuit crumb. The boy said, "That's a biscuit crumb," and swiftly ate it.

"Oh," said the bear. "Ah, hang on . . ." and he leaned his face close over the map, squinting hard at it and moving his head around, looking for something. With his nose so close to the paper he looked as if he were trying to sniff it out.

"Aha!" he cried, at last. "Here it is!" and he stabbed a claw at a spot in the top-right quarter. The boy followed the bear's claw down to the tip, beneath which he could just make out a tiny black speck.

"What's that then?" said the boy.

"It's a rock," said the bear. "So it's just as well we have the map so we can make sure not to hit it. That's the kind of responsibility a good captain takes very seriously, I'll have you know."

The boy was speechless. A single tear traced a route down his cheek.

"No need to cry with joy," said the bear. "It's all part of the service."

Message in a Bottle

The bear rowed. The boy sat very still and stared blankly out to sea. His stomach felt as if it was tightly knotted inside him and his mouth felt very dry. He drank the last of the ginger beer. It was flat and warm and horrible and he wished he had a dozen more bottles just like it.

Once, on holiday at the seaside, he had found a bottle on the beach with a message on a piece of paper inside it. It had come from another country: quite a long way away, his dad told him. He had meant to look it up on the map when he got home but he forgot and now he couldn't even remember the name of the country. It hadn't said anything very interesting (so far as they could tell), but he had been excited to think how far it had come to reach him. He decided to write a message of his own. He used the paper bag the sweets had been in and wrote on it with a pencil from his bag.

When he had finished, he put the paper into the bottle and screwed the top back on. Then he leaned out over the back of the boat and dropped the bottle into the water. He watched it, bobbing there on its side, growing smaller and smaller as they moved away from it. Soon it was just a speck in the distance. Then it was half a speck.

Then it was gone.

Smelly

Time passed. It got darker and a little colder but otherwise nothing much changed. The bear rowed. The boy fidgeted and fussed. He was stiff and restless and, despite his tiredness, longed for some activity. He wanted to stomp about impatiently but there wasn't room so all he could manage was some rather awkward shuffling and, still unused to the unsteadiness of the boat, he lost his balance. He lurched against the side and the boat tipped, sending him further off balance. He arched his back, windmilled his arms and just managed to stay upright. Not only that, but he was pretty sure that the bear, head down and concentrating on his rowing, hadn't noticed anything. Then the boat rocked back the other way and the boy fell, landing on his bottom with a loud thump.

"Having a lie down?" said the bear, still not looking up. But the moon was full and bright enough for the boy to see him smiling.

"Hmf!" said the boy.

The bear pulled his smile in at the sides a bit.

"You should get some sleep," he said. "It's late."

"I'm not tired," said the boy, sitting tenderly back on his seat. Then he yawned noisily.

"No, I can see that. Are you hungry, though? Do you want anything to eat? I think we'd better save the chocolate for now, but there's a sandwich left."

The bear stopped rowing and reached beneath him for his lunch box.

"I thought we'd eaten them all already," said the boy.

"I thought so too," said the bear, "but then I cleared out all the tin foil and found this one at the bottom of the box. I think it must be left over from my last trip. So it's, um, a bit past its best."

"What's in it?" said the boy. He had tried a few of the bear's sandwiches by now and had grown wary of their eccentric fillings. There had been: tuna fish, peanut butter and pineapple; sprout and honey; chilli pepper, mustard and horseradish; and what the bear called his "Breakfast

Special": bacon, sausage, egg, porridge, cornflakes and coffee beans between two slices of toast. He didn't relish the thought of anything else along the same lines. But he really was very hungry.

The bear rummaged in the lunch box and pulled out something bready and triangular. He held it towards the boy.

"All yours," he said.

The boy looked at the proffered sandwich. He noticed that the bear was holding it rather gingerly in the tips of two claws and right at the corner. Despite this, the bread did not bend at all. The boy looked up at the bear. He looked back at the sandwich. It was very difficult to tell what colour it was by moonlight, but whatever colour it was it didn't seem right.

"What's in it?" said the boy again.

"I can't remember," said the bear.

81

"Well, open it up and take a look," said the boy.

"I can't," said the bear. "It's stuck."

The boy looked up at the bear. The bear smiled thinly down at the boy. They both looked back at the sandwich.

"Is it . . ." said the boy.

"What?" said the bear.

"Is it . . . only a bit, but is it . . . *glowing?*"

"No," said the bear.

They each squinted at the sandwich and leaned in (cautiously) to look more closely.

"Hardly at all," said the bear.

"I'm not really that hungry," said the boy. "You have it."

"That's very kind," said the bear, "but I think that I'll save it for breakfast."

And when he put the sandwich away again the boy noted that the bear locked the lunch box, which he didn't usually do, and seemed to take extra care as he stowed it away.

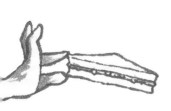

They each returned to their usual places.

"You should get some sleep," said the bear. "I'll keep going for a bit. It's a nice night. Thought I'd row for a while longer and take a look at the moon."

"Look at the moon?" said the boy. "Why? It's not going to do anything, is it? I mean, the moon is just the moon." But as he said it he looked up at the moon himself and, as there was nothing better to do, he kept looking at it for quite a while. He'd been right, it didn't do anything, but it didn't have to, it was just beautiful. It just was. The boy gazed at the moon, longer and harder than he ever had before (because who would spend time looking at the moon when there was a telly to watch and video games to play and comics to read?) and felt, for a moment, calm and safe and sure.

"Coo!" he said, but very quietly. And then the boy looked at the stars. There were a lot of them, more, he thought, than usual. He wondered where all the new ones had come from. Maybe they were just all the usual ones but they'd all bunched together in the same bit of sky. He twisted his neck looking up at different patches of sky, but they all seemed equally crowded.

"You can see more stars out here," said the bear, as if reading the boy's mind, "because it's properly dark."

The boy lowered his head and looked at the bear.

"It's funny, isn't it?" the bear went on. "With everything else you can't see as well in the dark, but with stars you can see them better. In towns, with streetlights and suchlike, it's not dark enough to see some

of them, but out here . . ." He looked up and smiled and either forgot to continue or felt no need. The boy looked up again too. They sat there for a while, quiet and content, drinking in the beauty of the bejewelled night.

"Do you use them to navigate by?" asked the boy.

"Eh?"

The boy looked at the bear, and his neck, stiffened by a light breeze, gave a small ache of complaint at having to move again.

"Do you use the stars to know which way to go?"

The bear scrunched his brow.

"To know which way is north and south and everything?"

"Ooh," said the bear, "that sounds clever. How do you do that?"

"I don't know," said the boy. "You're supposed to be the sailor. I don't even know the names of any of them."

"They have names?" said the bear.

The boy's wide eyes were like two more dim stars now, staring hard in disbelief.

"Yes, of course," said the boy. "They all have names. And if you know the names and you know which one is which and where they all go then you can tell which direction is which and know which way you need to go. Somehow."

"Coo!" said the bear. "That sounds like a lot of hard work when you could just use a compass."

"Have you got a compass?" said the boy.

"No," said the bear.

"So how do you know which way we're going?"

"I just do," said the bear. "I know where

we are and I know where we're going. And that's all, but that's enough."

The boy looked grumpy and suspicious. He was getting cold too. He hunted around huffily, feeling for his coat in the especially dark darkness beneath his seat.

"Oh," said the bear, "I do know one thing about telling directions from the stars."

"What's that, then?" said the boy.

The bear pulled his oars in and stood up, raising his eyes to the deep dark and the dazzle of the sky. He scanned the stars in the patch of sky directly above him, as if seeking something out. The boy stood too, up on top of the middle bench seat, closer to the bear than he normally ever got, to follow his gaze. He was still shorter than the bear, but he could look into his eyes now and see reflected in their dark wetness the wonder and magic and mystery of the night, the stars sparking and sparkling within. Then he looked up again, trying to see what the bear saw, searching the blinking lights as if for clues or patterns.

"You see . . ." said the bear, in a distant, quiet voice, as if almost in a trance. He slowly raised an arm.

"You see . . ." He pointed at the nameless stars above, ". . . those three brightest stars there, almost in a line?"

"Yes," said the boy, in a whisper, looking straight along the bear's raised arm and pointed claw.

"Well, that way . . ." said the bear.

"Yes?" said the boy.

"That way . . ." said the bear.

"Yes?"

". . . is definitely . . ."

"Yes?"

"Up," said the bear.

There was a long, long pause during which the boy considered a number of things to say to the bear. He came up with something quite good (and very rude), but was still waiting for the bear to stop sniggering naughtily at his own joke when he was overcome by a horrible feeling of nausea. The bear, still giggling, had not lowered his arm and the boy's face was close to his armpit.

"Aaaaaargh!" said the boy. "You stink!"

It wasn't as clever a thing to say as he'd intended but it worked rather well. The

bear looked hurt and the boy was glad of it.

"I've been working quite hard, you know," said the bear defensively, quickly lowering his arm. "I was bound to work up a bit of a sweat. I'm not surprised if I smell a little . . . ripe."

"Ripe?" said the boy, pinching at his nose and retreating to the back of the boat. "More like rotten! I think I'm going to be sick! Eurgh!" The boy leaned out of the boat and, overacting outrageously, pretended to be sick.

"Oh! Eurgh! S.O.S.! Mayday! I'm stuck on a boat with a fat, stinky bear! Bleurgh! Send help! Send the coastguard! Send soap!"

His already unconvincing act was made no more believable by frequent bouts of laughter. Even without looking back, the boy could tell that the bear was hurt, and he no longer took pleasure in the fact, but somehow, now that he had started laughing, he found that he couldn't stop. He slumped over the side and laughed and howled and beat his fists until he was breathless and hoarse and exhausted.

At last he stopped. He felt ashamed and didn't want to look round at the bear. But somehow, even now, he felt no urge to apologise. So he knelt there staring into the dark water and listening to his breathing and his heart, both slowing.

Suddenly the water lit up and the boy saw his reflection. There were tears on his cheeks and he didn't know if they were tears of laughter or of regret. Either way, he didn't want to look at himself, so finally he stood, embarrassed, still not facing the bear directly but glancing sheepishly at him out of the corners of his eyes. The bear had lit an old-fashioned lantern and was hanging it from a pole he had raised at the front of the boat. The bear sat down and took up his oars once more.

"You should sleep now," he said.

The boy turned away from him, lay down

and curled himself up beneath the ragged blanket that the bear had given him on the first night. He closed his eyes and listened to the rhythm of the oars.

Splish, splish, splish . . .

He wondered what he might say or do to apologise. But before he had thought of anything he was fast asleep.

Alone

The boy awoke. He had slept well but he still felt awful. His body ached from another night on wooden planks and his stomach was demanding to be fed, but most of all the boy felt bad about calling the bear smelly. He lay still for a moment, plucking up the courage to say sorry, trying to choose the kindest and best words. Once he was satisfied he'd got them right he started blurting them out as he uncurled himself from beneath the blanket and clumsily rose to his feet, rubbing the sleep from his eyes.

"Sorry I said that you stink, Bear. I mean, you do a bit, but it's not your fault and I bet there are bears that smell even worse. And I shouldn't have pretended to be sick because you didn't really make me want to be sick. Much. Hardly at all. And, anyway, it's not really your fault. I guess all bears smell a bit stinky, I'm just not used to it. And I guess when you're a bear yourself you don't really notice it so . . ."

He was standing now and facing forward. The bear wasn't there.

Ridiculously, the boy looked behind himself. Then he stared forward again, making absolutely sure. The bear really wasn't there. The oars were pulled in and his seat was empty. And in every direction (and the boy checked all of them at least twice) there was nothing to be seen except sea and sky. He found the bear's telescope and checked again, but it made no difference.

In a daze, the boy slumped down onto his seat, his eyes wide with shock and disbelief. Perhaps the bear had been eaten up by a sea monster and the boy had slept through the whole thing. How awful! But, no, that couldn't be it, there weren't really any sea monsters. It was just something the bear had made up, wasn't it?

Maybe he'd been kidnapped by pirates. They still existed, apparently. The boy had seen it on the news. They didn't have eye patches, wooden legs or parrots these days, but they were still pirates, apparently. And they were definitely baddies. But surely the bear would have put up a fight. And pirates fighting a bear – that would have to be pretty noisy. The boy was sure he would have woken up.

So the bear must have just abandoned ship to teach the boy a lesson. Either he'd got so angry he'd just swum off or . . . the boy could hardly stand to think the thought but it wormed its way into his head just the same. Maybe the bear had been so upset and angry that he'd drowned himself! Surely he couldn't be that sensitive? Bears aren't sensitive, are they? But he definitely wasn't there and the boy had ruled out monsters and pirates . . .

The boy felt a lot more awful now than he had done when he woke. He hadn't been happy to be stuck on a small boat in the middle of nowhere with a big, smelly bear, but it was a lot better than being stuck on a small boat in the middle of nowhere entirely on his own. And even if the bear

was irritating and smelly and infuriating, the boy still quite liked him really. Mostly. The boy felt at once as if he were entirely empty and as if he might explode. His head felt sick and his stomach felt dizzy.

Tears and rage and sadness welled within him and he knew that at any moment they would all start pouring noisily out of him.

Then with a wet *Splop!* a large sponge landed at his feet. The boy stared at it. Then he stared at the bear, bobbing in the water a few feet from the bow.

"I brought you a present from the bottom," he said. "Have you seen a real live sponge before?"

The boy was so amazingly relieved to see him that, naturally, all he could do was shout angrily.

"What do you think you're doing? You were gone for ages! I didn't know where you were! Do you know how worried I've been?"

Then he shut up, partly because he sounded exactly like his mum (and when she said those things he always told her not to make a fuss) and partly because he suddenly needed to concentrate on not falling over. The bear was climbing back into the boat which dipped sharply to one side as a result.

"I thought you'd be pleased," said the bear, rather tetchily, as he flopped wetly over the side. "I was having a bath so as to be more fragrant to your delicate young nostrils, but I can see the effort has gone unappreciated. *And* I dived right down to the bottom to get you that sponge. That's not easy you know. Luckily I'm good at holding my breath." The bear struck what was meant to be a heroic pose, but it was rather undermined by his petulance and the way his fur looked funny when it was wet. "Big lungs," he said, proudly, as puddles formed at his feet and drew watery lines along the cracks between the planks.

"Aren't you meant to be rowing this thing," said the boy. It was meant to sound angry but he was smiling a little as he said it.

Inclement Weather

The bear rowed and the boy sat. The boy wasn't sure at first if he could even be bothered with his usual morning look around. But then he didn't really have anything better to do, and he had a long day to fill. So he stood and stretched and looked out over the back of the boat and away to each side and saw only a cloudless blue sky over a featureless blue sea.

He decided to take the forward view by surprise. He braced himself, hunched his shoulders, scrunched his eyes shut and crouched just a little as he counted silently to three. And then he pounced! He whirled around, jumping on the spot and turning himself to face forward, opening his eyes wide and shouting, "HAH!" just for good measure.

The bear, who had been in his usual happy daydreaming state as he rowed, leaped inches from his seat in surprise. Then, as he bumped back down, he lost his stroke. One of the oars came up out of the water and skimmed over the surface while the other dug too deeply in. He hit himself hard in the belly with the handle of the one oar, knocking the breath from him, while the other came loose from his grip. He doubled over in pain, but quickly sprang back up to catch at the loose oar as it slid away. Flustered, he lunged at it clumsily, doubling himself over once again and just managing to catch it in time.

Still hunched over, and a little winded, he looked up at the boy, angry words gathering behind his teeth jostling to get out. But he saw that the boy had a surprised expression on his face and was pointing over the bear's head at something. He looked round.

There was a cloud.

It wasn't a big cloud. It wasn't an interesting shape. It wasn't beautiful. But it was there, breaking the monotony of the sky, a light grey blot amid the flat blue. It was something different, and it had surprised and pleased the boy because of that.

The bear threw it a glance and then mustered a scowl for the boy. Then he started rowing again and cheered up almost instantly.

They were rowing straight towards the cloud and as the day passed it grew slowly bigger and darker.

"It looks like a storm coming," said the boy.

The bear turned for a fresh look.

"No, not a storm," he said. "It might get a bit . . . inclement. Perhaps a drop or two of rain. But not a storm, no."

Half an hour later, hard rain lashing at his face, the boy took this up with the bear.

"I thought you said there wasn't going to be a storm," he shouted.

The bear gave him a puzzled look.

"This? This isn't a storm," he said. "This is just a bit of rain."

The *Harriet* leaned over alarmingly as a wave struck it hard on one side. The bear casually dipped an oar into the water, turning them to ride more comfortably over another even larger wave.

"But it's all wrong!" said the boy.

"What do you mean?" said the bear.

"Rain is meant to go this way," said the boy, waving a frantic hand straight up and down. "Not this way!" Now he waggled the same hand horizontally.

"Ah, yes. There is a bit of a breeze too, now you mention it," said the bear.

The boy gave him an exasperated stare.

The bear stared firmly back.

"I've been in storms, lad," he said. "I've been in real storms. And this isn't one, believe me."

The boy said nothing more. He was still annoyed, but he could see that the bear was genuinely untroubled by the conditions. He steered the boat expertly, riding the waves with ease, showing little more concentration or effort than when the waters were calm. He knew what he was doing.

"Don't worry," he said. "This is just a little squall." He glanced up and around, seemingly oblivious to the lashing rain and the biting wind. "It'll soon be . . ."

With eerie suddenness the rain stopped, the clouds dissolved and the sea flattened.

". . . over," said the bear.

The boy wiped a hand across his face, clearing wet hair from his eyes, and looked round in amazement. In all directions he saw a clear blue sky over a calm blue sea. It was as if the squall had never happened. He almost wondered if he had dreamed the whole thing. Only the ankle-deep water in the bottom of the *Harriet* (with the rubber duck now floating on top of it) told him otherwise.

After the bear had filled his water bottles from the rainwater (and they had both taken a long drink) the boy borrowed the kettle to bail with, and a warm sun set about drying out their sodden clothes and fur.

"See," said the bear, his snout turned up to the sky and a happy grin on his face. "It's turned out lovely."

The boy, tired and wet and hungry, didn't quite agree. But then they shared the last of the chocolate and he cheered up a bit.

He looked through the comic again. He had it out on the middle bench to dry and had to turn its soggy pages very carefully to avoid pulling them free from their staples. It took him a long time to get to the end this way.

And then, of course, the end wasn't the end anyway.

The Very Last Sandwich

They had been trying to ignore it for quite some time, but the noise their stomachs were making was getting so loud now that each was struggling to hear what the other was saying. It was as if, while the boy and the bear attempted polite conversation, their digestive systems were having an increasingly heated argument.

At last, the boy dared to broach the subject.

"I'm hungry," he said, and his stomach growled a low note of agreement.

"Really?" said the bear.

"Is there anything left at all?" said the boy.

"Well, we had the last of the chocolate . . ."

"So there's nothing?"

"Well . . ."

The boy, whose expression was already downcast, cast it deeper.

"We're starving hungry," he said. "We're lost . . ."

"We're not lost!" said the bear.

". . . and there's no food left."

"Well . . ." said the bear.

"What?" said the boy.

". . . there's still . . ."

"Oh, no!" said the boy, "Not that! Not . . ." He could barely say the words. The

116

very thought of it made him feel sick and small and scared. "Not . . ." his voice was a whisper, ". . . The Very Last Sandwich!"

"Well, look, I know it doesn't look very appetising. . ." said the bear.

"Noooooo!"

"I know it's a bit . . . past its best."

"No way!" said the boy.

"And I suppose it does smell a bit funny. And there's a little bit of mould on it."

"A bit? It's furrier than you are!"

"It's not that bad," said the bear, not altogether convincingly.

They sat in awkward silence for a moment. Then their stomachs, presumably worried by the embarrassing break in the conversation, started moaning again with renewed vigour, the bear's a deep rumble, the boy's singing a harmony higher up the musical scale.

"I suppose it couldn't hurt to take a look at it at least," said the boy. "Where's the lunch box?"

"That's the spirit," said the bear, rummaging purposefully in the small storage area under his seat.

The boy watched the bear's bottom, stuck up in the air as he leaned over to search for the lunch box. He had noticed that the bear's tail was a handy indicator of his mood and he was relieved to see that it was waggling in quite a perky fashion now. It seemed as if the bear's confidence and optimism were genuine rather than just a reassuring act. The bear hummed as he rummaged and his bottom danced, just slightly, in time with the tune. Yes, for all the worrying details of their situation, the bear seemed genuinely to believe that they would be OK. So maybe they would. The boy managed a half-smile (he would save the other half for later) and glanced up at the cloudless blue sky, feeling anew the warmth of the sun on his face. *Yes*, he told himself, *everything will be fine.*

And he truly believed it.

"Ah!" said the bear.

"What?" said the boy, lowering his eyes and noting that the bear's backside was now worryingly still.

"Oh!" said the bear.

"What is it?" said the boy.

The bear straightened up and turned slowly to face the boy, holding open in front of him the old and battered metal lunch box. It had some new dents in it and it was empty.

"I think it's escaped!" said the bear.

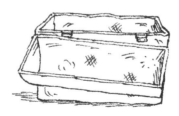

Fishing

They didn't spend long looking for The Very Last Sandwich and they didn't look very hard. The bear took a quick glance through the jumble and clutter at the front of the boat. The boy peered briefly into the shadows at the stern. Just for a moment he thought he heard something, a sort of wet crunching sound. Then he told himself very firmly that he had not and turned to face the bear.

"Well," said the bear, "as we're all out of

sandwiches, I suppose we'd better catch some fish."

"Oh, right," said the boy. He was rather thrown by this seemingly obvious solution to their food problem. He looked out at the sea and considered it in a new light. So far, he had only really thought of it as a kind of prison. And he had only thought of its surface, never of its depths and all the incredible varieties of life it contained. All its incredible varieties of tasty and nutritious life . . .

"Mmm . . ." he said, "a nice bit of fish . . . that'd be lovely. And I suppose you can just reach down into the water and scoop them up with your bare paws, can you?" (He had seen something of the kind on the telly once.)

"I wouldn't have thought so, no. But we could have a go with this."

122

The boy looked round at him and saw that the bear was holding a fishing rod. It was old and worn and a good length of the line had unravelled from the reel and tangled around it, but it looked sturdy enough.

"A passenger left this on board a couple of months ago. He got a bit seasick and left in a hurry when we got back to land . . . eventually. I've been meaning to give it the heave-ho for ages, but I'm glad I didn't now."

"Oh, good," said the boy, a tiny hiccup of hope making his voice sound odd. His next meal still seemed a long way off but at least he could believe there might be one now.

The bear examined the fishing rod, unknotting the tangled line and winding it back onto the reel. When he was finished he held up the free end.

"Hmm . . . no hook."

The boy, for once, was not discouraged.

"Maybe we could make one somehow."

"Yes," said the bear thoughtfully, "maybe, if I can find some wire or—"

The boy interrupted him. He had had an idea and he thought it might be a good one.

"Ah!" he said, scooping up the comic. "How about this?"

The bear looked puzzled. It was an expression

he had worn often over the years and it suited him rather well.

The boy was busy and intent. He opened up the comic and began working at one of the staples, unbending its arms and wiggling it free of the pages. He soon had it loose and held it up, proudly and hopefully, for the bear to see.

The bear gave it some thought.

"Yes," he said at last, "that could work." He plucked the staple from the boy's hand.

"Thank you," he said. Then, head cocked to one side, tongue out and eyes fixed in intense concentration, with surprising dexterity he used his claws like a pair of pliers to fold and bend and twist the staple into a neat hook shape.

"You're welcome," said the boy as the bear held up the end result.

"Now, what can we use for bait? Maybe

we need to have another look for that sandwich," said the bear.

"No," said the boy. "Not only do I not want to eat that sandwich, I don't want to eat anything else that's eaten that sandwich. Besides, at this stage I think the sandwich is more likely to eat the fish than the other way round."

"Hm. You do have a point," said the bear.

They thought for a while to the accompaniment of their duetting stomachs.

"Ooh!" said the bear. "We could make a fly."

It was the boy's turn to look puzzled. He wasn't as good at it as the bear but it was a decent enough effort for a beginner.

"You know," said the bear. "Fly fishing. They wear those really long wellies and stand in rivers for days on end. For fun.

And they use pretend flies for bait. Hooks made to look like insects."

A dim memory of a chilly visit, some years previously, to Boring Uncle Iain's house coughed politely for attention at the back of the boy's head.

"Oh, yes," said the boy. "I think I know what you mean. Aren't they usually a bit sort of hairy or feathery or, um . . . furry?"

"Yes. That's right. Now if we could just find some— OW!"

The bear scowled at the boy and rubbed an angry paw vigorously over the tiny patch on his thigh that suddenly found itself bald. The boy, trying quite hard to look apologetic rather than amused, held aloft the newly liberated tuft of fur between his thumb and forefinger.

"Yes," said the bear, snatching it away, "that should do."

He didn't stay angry at the boy for long. He was soon absorbed in the task of making the fly. It took a long while to work it out and the boy kept asking questions. But then sometimes, though he would never admit it, answering an annoying question helped him to work out what to do next. And making the fly was a fiddly business, so the boy's thin fingers were a help whenever two paws didn't seem enough to get the job done. After a lot of false starts, mistakes, a bit of shouting and a couple of minor puncture wounds, they managed between them to bind the tuft of fur to the hook using a loose piece of thread from the sleeve of the boy's coat. The bear licked his wounds while holding up the fly in the other paw. He and the boy scrutinised their handiwork.

"It looks good," said the bear.

"Yes, it does," said the boy.

He smiled at the bear. The bear smiled back.

"Let's catch some fish, then," he said.

The boy had an old door key that he took from his key ring to tie to the end of the line as a weight. The bear tied the rubber duck a few metres further up the line as a float. The newly furry hook went between the two, closer to the key than the duck.

"Is that right, do you think?" asked the boy, looking at it all.

"Right enough, I reckon," said the bear cheerily, and drew the rod back behind his head, then threw his arm forward, whipping the rod up and over with elegance and force, as if he'd been doing it all his life.

Then, after they'd carefully removed the hook from his bottom and he'd stopped yelling, he tried again.

The line flew out across the water,

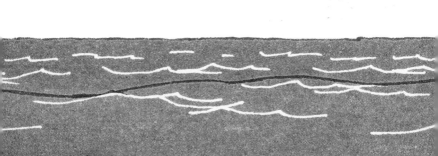

drawing an elegant arc through the air. The key hit the surface with a distant *plop* and pulled the hook down after it. The duck float floated and the line dropped down across the sea between it and the boat, doodling lazily across the surface of the water. The bear reeled in the line a touch, taking up the slack. Then they watched the distant duck bobbing on the sea. And they watched and they waited. And they waited and they watched.

A lot of time passed very slowly.

The boy's legs began to ache so he sat down. Then after a while his bottom ached from sitting on the hard wooden seat so he stood again. His stomach gurgled and he yawned.

"Shh!" said the bear, who had remained absolutely still (he hadn't even blinked) the whole time. "You'll scare the fish away."

"What fish?" said the boy (but very quietly). "I don't think there even are any."

"Of course there are fish," said the bear.

"Maybe our fly is no good after all," whispered the boy.

"It's a beautiful fly."

The bear still kept his eyes locked on the bobbing yellow duck and his voice was quiet and steady.

"The more I think about it, though," said the boy, "the more I think it didn't look all that much like a fly at all."

"Well, no," said the bear, "maybe not. But it doesn't need to look exactly like a fly."

"It didn't look anything like a fly."

"Well, no, not much. But it looks like some kind of an insect or something. That's good enough."

"What kind of an insect?" said the boy.

"I don't know," said the bear, a little sharply. "Maybe a caterpillar or something? Yes. It looks like a caterpillar. A bit."

"I suppose," said the boy and watched the duck for a while. It wasn't going anywhere.

"Do fish eat caterpillars?" said the boy.

"What?" said the bear.

"Do fish eat caterpillars?"

The bear thought about this.

"Yes. I think. Probably. Yes. Yes, I'm sure. Fish eat caterpillars. At least some kinds of fish eat caterpillars. At least some kinds of fish eat some kinds of caterpillars. Yes."

"Mm," said the boy.

A boringly gentle breeze thought about blowing, but decided in the end not to bother. That's how still it was. The duck just sat there. The boy was thinking.

"Wouldn't the fish that eat caterpillars," said the boy, "be in rivers though?"

"Maybe," said the bear, before, to be frank, he had given the matter any thought.

"Rather than out at sea," said the boy, "where there aren't any caterpillars."

"Um, maybe," said the bear. He stared out at the distant bobbing duck, floating on the water. A tiny bright spot on the vast dark sea. The boy stood beside him, facing the same way but not really looking at anything.

The boy gave the tiniest sniff.

"The fish out here probably never even

see a single caterpillar in their lives," he said.

"Well, that's good isn't it, because then they won't know that ours isn't a very good one, will they?" said the bear.

"I hadn't thought of that."

"And I don't think they have very good eyesight anyway, fish. And they're certainly not very clever."

"Hmm."

"And they probably get really bored of eating, um, whatever it is they usually eat. So if they see a caterpillar, even if they don't know what it is, they'll probably try eating it just for a change."

"I suppose," said the boy.

"So it'll be fine," said the bear. "At some point a shortsighted, stupid fish with a taste for adventure will come along and—"

The rod twitched. Their attention

snapped to the duck just as it disappeared beneath the water. With a flick of the wrist the bear jerked the rod sharply up and back, instantly pulling up the line and propelling out of the water and into the air a very startled fish. It flew through the air and landed neatly at their feet, flapping and bucking and bouncing around on the bottom of the boat.

"There. What did I tell you?" said the bear, and the boy couldn't help grinning with relief. He was almost laughing in fact. He felt a giggle rising inside him as he watched the bear take the hook from the fish's mouth. It wasn't a huge fish but it was big enough.

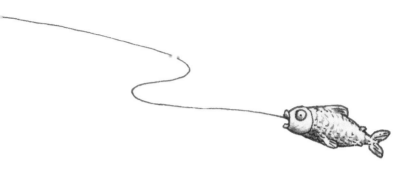

The boy wanted to dance with joy (but if he did then the boat would rock and he'd probably fall over, so he didn't).

THWACK!

The bear whacked the fish's head firmly against the side of the boat, just once, killing it instantly and knocking the boy's delight out of him, leaving him silent and wide-eyed with shock. The bear looked, oddly, both comical and menacing, standing there tensed from the excitement and holding a limp fish in one paw. The boy looked at him and said nothing.

Then his stomach growled again.

"Well don't just stand there," said the boy. "We've got a fish to cook."

Trading Up

The boy awoke and licked his lips. There was the slightest taste of yesterday's fish still on them and even that faint trace was exquisite. The bear had fried the fish in a small pan on his tea-making stove (lit, as ever, at arm's length and with comically extreme care) and they had eaten it with their fingers (and paws), the juices dripping messily down their faces, each of them rapturous at their release from hunger and at the glorious deliciousness of the fish. If their stomachs could have danced for joy they would have.

Then, for a little while, they had sat happily in the moonlight and talked and joked. The bear had even tried to teach the boy a sea shanty, but it seemed to the boy that the tune kept changing each time the bear sang it and then, when the boy finally thought he'd got a grip on the melody, the bear would lose his way on the ukulele or forget the words and bring the song to a stuttering halt for a while. Then he would begin again, in a different key, possibly on a different song entirely, it was hard to tell. It was an awful racket, to be honest, but their laughter sounded sweet enough in the pauses. And at some point the boy had fallen asleep and slept more deeply and dreamed more happily than ever he had since they had set off.

Now the taste of yesterday's meal on his lips roused his hunger. His stomach grumbled. Yesterday's fish had been amazingly tasty, but it hadn't been so very big. And it had been yesterday. The boy's stomach, having been reminded what it was there for, was keen to get back to work. The bear's was clearly thinking along the same lines. It rumbled deeply. The boy's tummy gurgled a harmony.

"You can take a turn with the fishing rod if you like," said the bear. "See if you can catch us something. I'm going to keep rowing."

The boy was quite excited at the prospect of fishing. He'd never really seen the appeal before when he'd seen grown-ups doing it for fun (how was it fun, sitting very still for a long while with nothing happening?), but now that it was a way of not starving to death he began to see the point of it.

His first attempts at casting the line didn't go too well. With one try he managed to get the hook caught in his coat, which was scrunched up on his seat, and hurl it out into the water. Another time he tangled the line around one of the oars and set the bear growling at him for interfering with his rowing. Eventually, though, the boy realised that he could just lower the rubber duck into the water and then gradually unreel the line as the boat moved on. Once the duck was far enough

away that he couldn't easily see it, he would reel the line slowly back in and then start again. He did this again and again and, though he was disappointed each time he failed to catch anything, he found he was not especially frustrated. He was patient, more or less, and, though the bear had remained silent throughout, offering neither advice nor discouragement at any point, the boy sensed that he approved. The sky was as cloudless as ever, the sea was still and the only sounds were the *splish, splish, splish* of the oars and a pair of grumbling, rumbling stomachs, but the boy was not bored. He was doing a job to the best of his ability. The sun was warming, the breeze was fresh. He felt good. Very, very hungry, but good: peaceful, contented, calm.

And then the duck ducked.

"Oooooooh!" said the boy.

"Aaaaaaaah!" said the boy.

"Whuthurr-ab-ab-ab-ab-ah-fuuuuh!" said the boy to the bear as he pointed at the spot where the taut fishing line met the surface of the water, the bull's-eye in a target of ripples.

The bear watched the boy with calm amusement, slowing the pace of his rowing but saying nothing. The boy turned his attention back to the fishing line, pulled back hard on the rod and began winding the reel. It wasn't easy. The tension in the line was tremendous. He sat down on the middle bench (squelching onto his coat that he'd laid out to dry there) and braced his feet against the rear seat. The rod bucked in his hands, as if trying to wrench itself free and leap into the sea, but the boy held it firmly, heaved back on it, saw it bend alarmingly above his head. He wondered if it might break in two, or else, surely, the line would snap.

"I think you've got something there," said the bear, enjoying himself.

The boy ignored him. Another hard tug on the line kept his attention focused there. The pull on the line had dragged the angle of the rod back down, close to horizontal, and the handle of the reel had slipped from his hand. The reel span as line flew out of it and the boy's unseen adversary raced away from the boat.

"Oh no you don't."

The boy grabbed at the handle, first

slowing the turn of the reel and then stopping it. He jerked the rod back again, pulling the line tight, then lowered it back down while reeling in line to maintain the tension. He'd seen this done somewhere, he thought. He didn't think he was doing it quite right, but he won back some of the lost line just the same. He did it again: pulled back; lowered; reeled in. It was smoother this time. As he pulled back a third time it was easier, the line was fighting him less, the rod bending more gently, as whatever he had caught grew tired. Soon he was able to reel the line in freely, turning the handle easily and quickly, grinning delightedly in anticipation. The angle of the line steepened as the catch was pulled closer and closer to the boat, the little yellow rubber duck speeding towards him across the water. Soon he would be lifting out his catch, triumphant. He realised that the boat was no longer moving and that the bear was standing behind him now, watching over his shoulder. The boy felt great. He wound and wound the reel, and watched as the fish finally emerged from the water and dangled, flipping and flapping in the air, at the end of the line.

It was tiny.

"Quite a fighter, that one, wasn't he," said the bear. But there was no mockery in his voice. He took the fish from the hook. It only took a small *thwack* to kill this one but the boy still winced a little.

"Well done," said the bear. "He's just the job."

"Don't be stupid," said the boy, grumpily. "He's much too small. Not much of a meal for either of us."

"That's true," said the bear, rubbing a

thoughtful claw beneath his snout. "But we're not going to eat this one."

Something about the bear's tone was making the boy nervous. And there was a look in his eyes too: he was staring a little too intently, but not exactly at anything, as if slightly in a daze. And his stance was too tense, as if his muscles had all clenched or he was full of electricity, as if there was something inside him waiting to get out.

"I've had," said the bear, "a brilliant idea."

Oh no, thought the boy.

"Oh yes?" said the boy.

"This fish," said the bear, lifting it delicately by its tail, "is too small for us to eat, but if we use it as bait . . ."

"Then we could catch a bigger one!" said the boy. He looked excited. Then he looked shocked. He stood very still with his eyes wide and his mouth hanging open,

and neither moved nor spoke for quite some time.

"What is it?" said the bear, waving a paw in front of the boy's staring eyes.

"That," said the boy, in a dazed, bemused voice, "really is a brilliant idea."

He turned his head to look up at the bear, addressing him directly.

"How did that happen?"

The bear made a show of taking offence at this, but only for a moment – he was too eager to put his plan into action to waste time on play-acting.

It took a bit of thinking (and then some doing) before they could start fishing again. The boy pointed out that to catch a bigger fish they would need a bigger hook, so the bear took a small nail (torn with his teeth from a wooden crate full of who knew what that he had stowed in the bows) and bent it into shape. Then he tied it to the line in place of the caterpillary-fly. Then he hooked it inside of the little fish and handed the rod back to the boy.

"I can't stand round here all day," he said. "I've got rowing to do. You can do the fishing again. You're clearly a natural."

The boy held back a proud grin as best he could and they resumed their positions.

The bear rowed. The boy dropped the line into the water. He played out a little line.

The duck sank almost immediately.

The fish must have been as surprised as the boy was. It barely put up any kind of a fight and was much easier to land than the last one, despite being bigger. Much, much bigger. The boy heaved it aboard. The bear took it from him (which was a relief) and held it up. They both looked at it with admiration and hunger.

"It's huge!" said the boy.

"Yes," said the bear, "it's a beauty."

"Shall I get the stove and the pan out?" said the boy, scuttling off to the front of the boat.

"Well," said the bear. *THWACK!* "We *could* cook this one. Or . . ."

The boy stopped in his tracks and felt the uneasy rocking of the boat beneath his feet as he looked back at the bear.

"Or what?" he said. "Were you thinking of having it stuffed and hung over your fireplace instead?"

"I don't have a fireplace," said the bear, missing the boy's sarcasm. "But what I was thinking was: if using a little fish as bait caught us a big fish . . ."

The boy could see where this was going (which admittedly made a pleasant change from everything else recently) and he didn't like it.

"Oh no," he said.

". . . then if we use a big fish as bait . . ." said the bear, carrying on regardless.

"No, no, no," said the boy.

". . . we could catch a really, really big fish which would keep us going for days," said the bear.

"I don't think the line could take the

weight of anything much bigger, though," said the boy. "Or the rod. Or my arms, for that matter."

"Hmm," said the bear. He put the big fish down and picked up the rod. He looked at the line. He looked at the rod, flexing it thoughtfully. He glanced briefly at the boy's arms.

"You're right," he said at last.

The boy brightened.

"We can't use the rod," said the bear, "so we'll need different tactics. Pass me the tool box, will you? The blue one, just by your foot there."

The tool box wasn't that easy to get at. Clearly it hadn't seen much use recently as it was covered in, and surrounded by, all sorts of other odds and bobs and bits and ends. The boy dug his way in and extracted it and lifted it onto the centre seat. The bear opened it up. The boy peered in.

It was a big box with a large number of different-sized compartments that opened up and spread out as the box itself was opened. All of them were empty except for the biggest section at the very bottom in which was a large wooden mallet.

"Is that it?" said the boy.

"All the tools I've ever needed," said the bear, contentedly, lifting the mallet from the box with one paw and tapping it heftily into the other, and gazing off into the distance and the past. "Used to work wonders on the engine."

"*Harriet* used to have an engine?"

"Yes," said the bear. "Briefly." He looked thoughtfully down at the mallet.

"They don't build them like they used to, you know. They really don't."

A moment passed.

"But what's that got to do with fishing?" said the boy, pointing at the mallet.

"Well," said the bear, "like you said, the rod and the line wouldn't take the weight of the kind of fish we're after now so . . . "

He stood at the back of the boat and held the fish out over the water in his left paw. In his right paw he gripped the mallet behind his back, poised and ready to swing.

"See?" said the bear. "The really big fish jumps out of the water to eat the quite big fish and then . . . POW!"

He waggled the mallet.

"Pow?" said the boy.

"That's right. POW! Then we'll have food for a week at least, I reckon. Brilliant, isn't it?"

The boy didn't think it was brilliant. He told the bear this quite clearly and politely, and then not quite so politely, and then

really very rudely. He strongly suggested that they cook and eat the fish they'd got right now. The bear was having none of it.

"It's the captain's decision to make," he said, tapping his captain's hat (not quite as lightly as he'd intended) with the mallet for emphasis. "Long-term planning, that's the thing," he huffed. "That's what captaincy is all about. But I wouldn't expect you to understand."

The boy rolled his eyes, but decided not to argue any further. The bear could stand there holding a fish all day so far as he was concerned. And once the bear finally gave up, at least they could cook and eat the fish they'd already got. And teasing the bear about it all afterwards would provide entertainment for days. He just hoped the bear wouldn't be too stubborn. Surely he would give up after an hour or two.

The boy made himself comfortable at the front of the boat. He started to read the comic again. He didn't pay it much attention though. He knew it so well now that there were no surprises left in it for him. He looked up at the bear, standing there, tongue out in concentration, fish clasped in one paw, mallet in the other. No surprises there either. Then he looked just at the fish and his stomach rumbled.

"Shh!" said the bear, without looking round. "You'll scare the fish away."

Before the boy could reply he was interrupted by a much lower, louder rumble that made the whole boat shake.

"I'll scare the fish away?" said the boy. "Your tummy's much worse than mine."

The bear looked puzzled.

"That wasn't my tummy," he said.

The rumble rumbled again. It was a terrible, low growling, even louder now, and the boat was pitching and rocking.

The bear, struggling to keep his balance, nevertheless still held the bait steady over the now choppy waters.

"That's odd," he said.

The growling got louder still, the

volume growing more quickly now. The boy looked all around, trying to work out which direction it was coming from. There was nothing to be seen. It made no sense. Louder still. He could feel the vibrations of it through the boards of the boat's hull, up through his feet and legs to shake his stomach. Deafening now, the sea around them foaming and angry. And then the boy realised.

"It's coming from underneath us!" he shouted to the bear.

"What?" said the bear, turning to look at the boy but still keeping his baited arm outstretched.

A huge column of water shot upward from the sea directly behind the boat, the tremendous noise of it combining with an unearthly growling, howling, thundering cry as something very big and very strange

burst out of the sea and neatly snatched the fish from the bear's hand. The boat was thrown up into the air, turned a neat somersault and landed back down on the water with a smack, knocking the boy and the bear over onto their backs. They looked up at the terrifying thing towering above them, at the many eyes, the tentacles, the barnacle-encrusted skin, the gaping mouth full of very big and very pointy teeth.

The boy screamed and turned his head away. But then he found himself staring at The Very Last Sandwich, lying next to his head, and screamed again even louder.

The bear rose slowly to his feet, looking up at the creature in awe.

"Ooh . . ." said the bear, "you really are a big fella!"

The strange thing arched its serpentine body to bring its head closer to the bear, all its many eyes staring straight at him with alien curiosity. The thing looked at the bear. The bear looked at the thing.

"Oh well," said the bear. "Made a plan. Better stick to it, I suppose." And with that, mallet in paw, he leaped from the boat.

The Thing From The Deep

The bear leaped straight at the thing's dreadful face, but the creature raised a swift tentacle from the water and struck the bear in the belly, batting him up into the air. He twisted his body as he flew upwards, turned a graceful loop and landed neatly on the thing's head. Then he started belting it with the mallet.

"Don't hit him!" shouted the boy. "Ask him if he knows the way!"

The bear stuck to his task, swinging the

mallet with all his strength repeatedly at the monster's head. He looked determined and angry.

"We . . ."

THWACK!

". . . are . . ."

THWACK!

". . . not . . ."

THWACK!

". . . lost!"

CRUNCH!

Splash!

"Oh," said the bear. The handle of the mallet had snapped with the last blow and the head of it had dropped into the water. So far as the bear could tell, the enormous, scary, dangerous monster did not seem to have become any less enormous, scary or dangerous as a result of being hit repeatedly on the head.

"Ah," said the bear.

"I think you've made it angry," shouted the boy. "That probably wasn't such a good idea."

"No," said the bear. "Probably not."

The thing reached up a slimy tentacle and made a grab at the bear. The bear twisted and ducked under it, but the slippery goo that oozed from the creature's skin made him lose his footing and slip from the top of its head. Thrashing his arms about as he fell, he managed to grab on to one of the beast's antennae. He had avoided falling off completely, but now he was dangling in front of the monster's massive face.

"Try to stay away from its mouth," shouted the boy helpfully. "I think it's still hungry."

"I'll bear that in mind," said the bear.

He gazed into the

monster's
many eyes. With
his free paw he gave it a
little wave.

The monster did not
wave back. Instead, it shook
its head, bouncing the bear
around at the end of the
antenna like a fish on the end
of a line. It opened its mouth
wide, exposing its countless
teeth and dribbling thick snotty
drool down its front. Its jaws
slammed shut again and again,
snapping at the bear as he swayed
and swung and bounced around
in the air, clinging on as best he
could as he twisted and bent his
body to keep clear of a toothy death.

"Coo, dear!" he said. "Your breath

smells rotten!"

And then, suddenly, the monster stopped thrashing about and remained for a moment perfectly still as it regarded the bear gradually swinging to a halt before its many, many eyes. The bear stared back unblinking with a faint, rather friendly, smile.

"Have you had enough now?" he said. "Do you give up?"

Something tapped him on the shoulder. He twisted round to see a gigantic, slimy tentacle poised in the air behind him, swaying a little from side to side, like a cobra waiting to strike.

"Oh dear," said the bear.

The tentacle lashed violently towards him but, rather than striking him, coiled around him, gripping him hard in a spiralling embrace from neck to toes.

"Oh!" said the bear.

The monster gave him a squeeze.

"Ow!" said the bear.

Then the creature raised the bear high into the air, tilted back its head and, after emitting a noise like a volcano laughing, dropped him into its mouth.

Then it spat him straight out again.

The bear flew through the air, foul-smelling gobs of thick spittle trailing in his wake, and landed with a splash some distance away.

The creature did not notice. It had turned its attention to the boat where the boy stood, rather nervously, holding the oar

with
which he
had just jabbed
the monster very
hard in its stomach.

It had seemed like a good idea at the time.

"Don't even think about it!" said the boy unconvincingly, wafting the oar in front of him rather limply while backing slowly and unsteadily away across the hull of the *Harriet*. The boat itself was moving away from the creature too, the prod of the oar having set it in motion.

The creature straightened itself, looming high above the boat, blocking out the sun and plunging the boy into gloom.

Still edging backwards, the boy peered up at its awful face. It was hard to read its expression (the boy was used to faces with far fewer eyes), but it seemed safe to assume that it wasn't happy. It raised two writhing, snaking tentacles high above the water and then brought them crashing down on either side of the *Harriet*.

The boat shot upwards on a plume of water, sending the boy flying onto his back, the oar dropping from his hands. The boy had scrambled halfway to his feet when two more tentacles smashed down into the water and another mighty wave shot the boat into the air. The boy, oars and everything else in the boat went flying. The boy landed hard on the bottom of the boat with oars and pans and stove and who knew what beneath and over him, and all of it in inches-deep water.

The sponge that the bear had brought up from the sea bed landed on his head and bounced away somewhere. For a moment nothing happened. The boy lay there, propped up on his elbows amid the chaos of scattered and battered belongings. He

tried to get up but banged his head against something. One of the oars had landed against the centre bench, its blade down in the bow section behind him, its handle up at an angle pointing at the beast. He had to wiggle around it as he got unsteadily to his feet, cautiously, half expecting the monster to toss the boat about some more. But it had tired of playing games now.

The creature arched its body, its mouth gaping wide, and issued a hideous roar that the boy could feel, like a stinky gale, as well as hear. Instinctively, he jumped backwards. One foot landed on the sponge, now saturated and slippery. His foot slid from beneath him and he toppled over, his full weight landing on the oar handle, smashing it downwards. The other end of the oar shot into the air, scooping up, as it did so, The Very Last Sandwich and shooting it over the sprawling boy. He watched it fly, as if in slow motion, curving through the air. It landed perfectly inside the gaping mouth of the sea monster. The beast gave an involuntary gulp and came to an instant halt.

The boy hauled himself half upright, watching. The monster was still and quiet. The boat rocked gently back to equilibrium. The boy could hear the faint splashing of the distant bear swimming towards the boat, but he didn't look round. Then there was a noise, a small noise, from somewhere deep inside the creature. It squinted one eye closed in discomfort but otherwise remained quite still. Then another noise, a little louder, a dull gurgling thud, like a small explosion. The closed eye opened and two other ones closed. A low rumble, and the beast's eyes bulged and its face puffed up. It opened its mouth and belched neatly, seemingly rather relieved. It just had time to turn its attention to the boy again before another rumble made its body shake. Then another, louder and longer, and the monster's eyes were shutting and opening madly, like lights blinking on and off. It groaned and closed all its eyes tight shut, as if concentrating hard. Somewhere very deep in the sea something went *boom* and the waters around the boat frothed with gigantic bubbles and the air filled with a terrible but familiar stench . . .

"Ooh," said the boy. "Disgusting!"

Then, after the briefest pause, the noises started up again. A continuous, thundering rumble grew steadily in volume, accompanied by a series of increasingly violent explosions. To this dark music the creature began to dance. It swayed and shook and jerked in time to the strange rhythms of its own insides, its movements becoming bigger and wilder as the noises grew louder, its tentacles thrashing crazily, slapping at the water in a terrifying frenzy, churning up the sea and pushing the little boat away at some speed. The boy looked on, fascinated and appalled. He dimly registered that the bear had climbed into the boat and joined him, watching the weird spectacle before them. The monster howled, a jagged, high-pitched, unearthly noise, adding to the general farting, thrashing, splashing fugue. Its body writhed, its tentacles flailed. The boat rocked and bucked and jumped, but its startled occupants kept their eyes steadily on the creature.

Then it stopped.

The banging and the booming and
the howling all ceased in an instant, and
the monster froze. The great tangle of its
tentacles made it look like a diagram of
a very complicated knot. It was strangely
beautiful. There was no sound except,
perhaps, a strange sigh.

Then it exploded, throwing out ragged

lumps of stinky, slimy flesh and drawing a pattern of splashes in a wide circle on the surface of the sea. The remains of its body folded in on itself, its tentacles wilted, and it sank slowly beneath the water.

"Do you think it was something he ate?" said the bear.

Floating Down

The boy and the bear tidied up the contents of the *Harriet* and, leaning over opposite sides of the boat, scooped up sea water and did their best to wash away bits of exploded monster. They were happy and relieved to be alive and they laughed and joked easily as if their recent ordeal had forged between them a strong, deep friendship.

This lasted about five minutes.

"You know, it was nice of you, but there

was no need to interfere like that," said the bear. "Defence of the vessel from sea monsters is really the captain's job and I had the situation completely under control."

"Under control?" said the boy.

"Yes. Of course," said the bear.

"Under control from inside that thing's mouth?"

"Um, yes," said the bear.

"So what, exactly, was your plan to escape?" said the boy.

"Oh, I didn't have a plan," said the bear. "I never have a plan. No point having a plan when you're a sea captain. When you're dealing with the sea you have to be able to adapt at a moment's notice. You have to deal with each situation as it arises. There's no point moaning about it, you just say: 'Here is where we are. What do we do now?' My dad taught me that. He was a sea captain too, you see."

The bear looked off to the horizon. Or perhaps to somewhere beyond it.

"Probably still is," said the bear. "Wherever he's got to."

The boy sighed.

"So, what would you have done, without a plan, to get free?" he said.

"I don't know. I was about to have a brilliant idea but I was interrupted," said the bear.

"Oh," said the boy, reaching down the neck of his T-shirt to extract a globule of pink blubber. "Another of your brilliant ideas?" He tossed the bit of monster into the water.

"Yes," said the bear.

"Only, your last 'brilliant idea' started with us having a fish to eat and ended with

182

us not having a fish to eat."

"Um . . ."

"Not to mention the nearly-getting-killed bit in the middle."

"Well," said the bear, "there's nothing wrong with *nearly* getting killed. *Actually* getting killed: now that would be annoying. But *nearly* getting killed is fine. I do it all the time and it's never done me any harm."

"Is that meant to make me feel better?"

"Yes," said the bear.

The boy's stomach interrupted with a loud grumble.

"Well, it doesn't. A nice big fish to eat might make me feel better, but we don't have one of those any more, thanks to you."

"We can catch another fish," said the bear.

"No we can't," said the boy. "The fishing rod's gone. It must have fallen out when the gigantic sea monster was playing pat-a-cake with the boat."

"Oh," said the bear. He looked a little concerned. "But we've still got the stove, haven't we?"

"Yes," said the boy. "But why do you care when we've got nothing to cook on it?"

"Well, it's almost four," said the bear.

"I can't believe," said the boy, "that you're worrying about tea."

The boy realised he was speaking quite loudly now. Not shouting exactly, but not far off. And he had climbed onto the central seat so that his face was almost on the same level as the bear's. And he was poking a finger into the bear's fur for emphasis.

Actually, he thought, *that's probably not a good idea. I should stop poking the bear.*

"Don't poke me," said the bear.

"I'll poke you if I want to," said the boy. He poked the bear again, hard, in the ribs.

I really wish I wasn't doing that, he thought.

"I won't warn you again," said the bear.

"You can't tell me what to do," the boy heard himself say. He watched his finger jabbing into the bear and wondered why it wouldn't stop.

"I'm the captain," said the bear. "I can order you to stop."

"Ha!" said the boy. "Some captain you are! Days at sea with no sign of land. No food. No idea where we are . . ."

"We are not lost!" shouted the bear.

". . . and your stupid hat doesn't even fit properly," said the boy.

His finger, like something that was no

longer a part of him, stopped poking at the bear and shot up as if to knock the hat from the bear's head. It didn't get there. The bear's paw grabbed his wrist and held it still with an uncomfortably firm grip.

"Don't you ever," growled the bear, "touch the captain's hat."

He stared angrily into the boy's eyes. The boy stared angrily back. He didn't want to but somehow he couldn't stop himself. *I should apologise,* thought the boy. *If I say the wrong thing now he might actually break my hand off. I should apologise. I'll apologise.*

"You're the worst captain ever!" said the boy.

Oh. That wasn't meant to happen, thought the boy. *That wasn't meant to happen at all.*

The boy found he was gazing off into the distance. He gulped and looked back to the bear, expecting to meet with a terrifying stare. But instead he found that the bear was looking up into the air between them. Something small and blue and fuzzy was there, falling slowly down. The boy lifted his head and focused on it, his eyes twitching as they followed its movements.

It was a feather. It rocked and turned and twirled and danced as it fell and the boy, hypnotised, slowly lowered his head as he followed its descent. It came to a stop on the tip of the bear's nose. The boy and the bear stared hard at the feather, the bear almost cross-eyed. They stared and they said nothing. They hadn't seen a bird in days. They stared at the feather, then they stared at each other, then they stared at the feather again. It was a beautiful thing, rich blue in colour, shiny and perfect, with a gentle curl to it. It sat on the bear's nose, basking in the afternoon light.

Then the bear sneezed, waking them both from their trance and shooting the feather back up into the air. They followed it with their eyes and then both looked beyond it, searching the sky.

"A feather!" said the boy.

"From a bird!" said the bear.

"Do you see it?" said the boy.

"No," said the bear.

"If we can spot it . . ." said the boy.

". . . We could follow it to wherever it's come from," said the bear. "There might be food there."

"Oh. I was just thinking we'd catch it and eat it."

"That's plan B. Do you see it?"

"No."

They stood there turning around and twisting their necks, searching the sky.

"There!" said the bear at last, pointing

very definitely at a particular patch of sky. The boy examined it closely.

"Where? I don't see . . . oh! Yes! Yes, yes, yes!"

The cloudless blue sky had a tiny dark speck in it.

"Well don't just stand there," said the boy. "Get rowing!" But when he looked down again he saw that the bear was already back in his seat, pulling hard on the oars, speeding them across the water.

Kark!

The bear rowed and the boy stood on his seat, keeping an eye on the bird. Now and then he would correct their direction with an urgent word to the bear or a gesture with his hand: "A little more to the left. *No,* my left! That's it." Even with all his effort the bear could not row the *Harriet* as fast as a bird can fly, but luckily this particular bird seemed content to dawdle. Sometimes it would circle around for a while and they would catch up on it, the dark speck growing bigger and occasionally catching the sunlight, flashing a startling iridescent blue. At one point it dived down into the water and the boy lost sight of it for long frightened seconds before it rose again into the air. They were close enough that the boy could just make out that it had a fish in its beak.

"Good," said the bear. "The extra weight might slow him down." He glanced over his shoulder to check their progress without breaking the rhythm of his stroke. "Good," he said again.

He was right. The bird slowed and, increasingly often, it paused and spent time circling in the air before setting off again on a slightly different course. They drew closer and closer to it, the boy seeing it ever more clearly, but there was still no

sign of anything on the horizon to indicate
that it was heading for land.

"It seems to be looking around," said
the boy, "trying to work out which way to
go. Maybe it's lost too."

"We're not lost!" said the bear. "And I
don't think that bird is either. Now tell me:
am I heading straight towards it?"

The boy said nothing, but indicated with an outstretched arm a minor adjustment in their course to starboard. The bear gave a more powerful stroke to his right oar than the left and the *Harriet* shifted direction perfectly. The boy gave the bear a nod of approval which, just for a second, took his eyes off the bird. He looked back up and

found it again instantly but, oddly, though they were closer now, it was harder to see. The bright blue was not so bright now. But it was too early in the day for the light to be fading. He squinted at the bird and rubbed his eyes.

"What's wrong?" said the bear.

"I don't know," said the boy.

The bird was a vague blue smudge now.

"I think there's something wrong with my eyes," said the boy. He sounded scared.

The bear looked round, spotted the bird and carried on rowing.

196

"Your eyes are fine," he said.

"Then why . . . ?" the boy trailed off.

"Mist," said the bear.

It fell quickly and thickened. After so many clear days with nothing to look at, here was a mist to hide their first glimpse of hope. The air turned cold around them in an instant and the blue smudge of bird dissolved before the boy's eyes. The bear kept rowing.

"Which way?" he said.

"I'm not sure," said the boy, staring as hard as he could, casting his eyes round this way and that. He caught a glimpse of colour and raised a straight arm towards it.

"There!" he said.

The bear adjusted his stroke, steered the boat round as instructed and powered on. But the mist grew thicker still and the boy lost sight of the bird again.

"I can't see it!"

"Just keep looking!"

"I *am* keeping looking. You keep rowing!"

"I'm rowing. Does it look like I'm not rowing?"

"I don't know, I'm not looking at you."

"Well does it sound like I'm not rowing?"

"All right, all right. Shut up and let me concentrate!"

The boy turned and twisted, but it was no use. He could hardly even see the bear now.

"I can't see it. Stop rowing!"

"Stop rowing? First you say 'Keep rowing,' now you say 'Stop rowing.' Make your mind up!"

"Stop rowing!" said the boy.

"Well if you're just going to give up . . ."

"And shut up!" said the boy.

The bear stopped rowing and shut up. The boy was right. There was no point just carrying blindly on. They might be heading away from the bird for all they knew. The mist covered everything. He looked at the faint shape of the boy still standing poised and alert on his seat. Even now the bear could tell that he was concentrating very hard. But why? There was no way that he could see anything.

"*Kark!*" said the bird.

It was a faint noise, but not so faint that they couldn't tell roughly which direction it had come from. The bear set off again.

They went on, neither saying a word.

"*KARK!*"

"That's close," said the boy, "and straight ahead!"

"Straight ahead it is," said the bear.

The boy couldn't see anything now, but he could feel how fast they were going. The bear was sending them along at a tremendous pace.

"Now we're getting somewhere!" said the bear.

And the boy was about to reply when –

BUMP!

"Oh!" said the boy.

"Oof!" said the bear.

"Ow!" said the boy.

And then no one said anything for a while.

The Mermaid

The boy awoke.

For a moment he couldn't remember where he was. Then he remembered that he was in the boat, but couldn't remember having gone to sleep. But he was lying down in his usual spot between the rear and centre seats and he had just woken up, so he must have gone to sleep. But he couldn't remember. And there was something else wrong.

"Ow!" he said again. And that reminded him.

"How's your head?" asked the bear, standing over him with a cup of tea as the boy delicately raised himself up from the deck.

"It feels like it's full of bees," said the boy.

"You should be more careful," said the bear. "You went flying into my belly and then bashed your head on the deck after you'd, uh, bounced off. You could do yourself a serious mischief jumping about like that."

"I wasn't jumping about! I fell off," said the boy. "You should be more careful and look where you're going."

"I couldn't look where I was going, could I? We couldn't see anything!" said the bear. "Because of the mist. Remember?"

"Well that's no excuse for bumping into . . ."

The boy looked at the bear.

"We bumped into something!" said the boy.

"Yes," said the bear.

"What did we bump into?" said the boy.

"See for yourself," said the bear, waving a paw over his shoulder.

The boy looked up past the bear and through the thinning mist at a dark looming shape close behind him.

"It's a ship!" said the boy.

"Yes it is," said the bear, sipping from his cup.

"Well, are we going on board then?" said

the boy. "What are we waiting for?"

The bear lifted his cup.

"I'm just finishing my tea," he said. He took another sip. "And I've shouted 'Ahoy!' and nobody's answered. The crew are either very rude or . . ."

"Or what?" said the boy. "Or deaf?"

"No," said the bear.

"Or very, very shy?" said the boy.

"No," said the bear. "I don't think there *is* anyone on board."

"Well then," said the boy and he pushed past the bear, picking his way past the gas stove and teapot on the floor, leaned over the side and reached out a hand towards the ship. "Look, there's a rope here we can climb up."

"At least, no one *alive*," said the bear. "I think it might be . . ."

"What?" said the boy.

"… a ghost ship," said the bear.

"That's ridiculous," said the boy, but it came out sounding strange because he shivered as he said it. He looked up at the ship. It did look creepy. And it was very old, old enough to be in a museum rather than out at sea. Its sails were tattered and its rigging looked like spiders' webs. Faded, flaking painted lettering spelled out the ship's name, *The Mermaid*, on its prow beside a carved wooden mermaid figurehead, her face worn almost featureless by many years of sea and weather. But, more than how it looked, there was something the boy felt, something deep inside his otherwise empty stomach, something wrong.

The boy's hand wavered in the air, just short of the dangling rope. The gentle rise and fall of the waves rocking the

Harriet tipped the boy's arm sometimes towards and sometimes away from the ship. A slight breeze pushed the rope and set it in motion, its free end swinging in a slow circle. Hand and rope moved back and forth and round and round, dancing a strange dance together without ever quite touching. The boy watched them, mesmerised, forgetting altogether that the hand was his own and that he could pull it away at any time and stick it safely in his

pocket. He was fascinated and petrified, wondering what would happen if the hand were to touch the rope. Maybe if anything living touched anything ghostly then it died. Could that be right?

"*Kark!*" said the bird.

207

The boy and the bear looked up and saw a bright blue shape perched in the rigging of the mainmast, looking very much alive.

The rope brushed against the back of the boy's hand. Nothing bad happened. The boy grabbed the rope, pulled it towards him, took hold with the other hand too and stepped up onto the side of the *Harriet*.

"I suppose you thought you'd scared me," he said to the bear, "but I'm climbing on board." With that, he lifted his feet and swung the short distance to the ship. His feet hit the side with a reassuringly unghostly thud, and he began to climb the rope.

Only he couldn't.

The boy had seen loads of films where heroes climbed up ropes and it always looked really easy, but he'd never actually done it himself. It turned out it wasn't easy at all. Especially when sea spray had made both the rope and the side of the ship wet and slippery. His feet slid down and it was all the boy could do not to fall off entirely. He dangled there for a while feeling equally scared and silly, his feet just above the water.

"Take your time," said the bear, eventually. "No rush."

"Oh shut up and help me out here," said the boy.

"Righto," said the bear. He swallowed the last of his tea and put down the empty cup. Then he took hold of the boy and lifted him effortlessly back into the little boat.

The boy grabbed the rope again. "You could climb this, couldn't you? You'll have a good grip if you dig your claws in."

"Maybe," said the bear, "but I'm not happy going aboard uninvited. It's rude to go aboard another captain's vessel uninvited."

"But if you think there's nobody on board then how can you be invited? In fact, if there's nobody on board then maybe, as a fellow captain, you should go aboard just to make sure the ship is all right. As a favour."

The bear glanced up at the ship and then back at the boy. He looked like he was thinking. And then he looked resigned. And then he looked determined.

"You're right."

"I am?" said the boy.

"Yes. We have to go aboard. You can climb onto my back and I'll carry you up. Here, tie us to the ship, I need to grab a few things."

The bear handed the boy the end of a short coil of tatty rope and began to stuff some things into his suitcase. He was busy and efficient now that the decision was made. The boy looked up again as he tied the bear's rope to the ship's rope. The mist had risen enough for him to have a clear view of the ship now, but a few foggy tendrils remained, clutching at the upper parts of the masts like the fingers of a giant ghost. He finished off a messy knot joining the two ropes, quickly attached the free end to the *Harriet* and gulped down his fear.

"Come on," said the bear. He was standing right in front of the boy with the suitcase in one paw. He turned around and crouched a little. The boy climbed onto the seat and from there jumped up onto the bear's back, wrapping his arms around

his neck.

"Hold on tight," said the bear, and the boy did as he was told. The bear put the handle of the suitcase between his teeth, leaped nimbly from the side of the boat, neatly caught hold of the rope and climbed straight up it as effortlessly as walking along a pavement. The boy clung to his neck, dangling and swaying as the bear raced upwards. Then all at once they were over the rail, the bear landing elegantly on his feet, the boy losing his grip and sprawling on the deck. He got up and took a deep, calming breath as he looked around. There was no sign of life on the

deck but there was no sign of anything dangerous or scary either. Just nothing. And no one. Aside from the blue bird, quietly watching them from its place in the rigging, the ship seemed entirely deserted. There was no sound either, except for the lapping of the water far below them and the faint snuffling of the bear sniffing inquisitively at the air.

"What can you smell?" said the boy.

"Only the sea," said the bear, his eyes hard and serious; then with a smile and a glance towards the boy, "and exploded monster. You need to wash your clothes you know. Come on then, this way." He strode off towards the rear of the ship. "The captain's cabin will be in the aft, I should think. We should see if he's home."

"Doesn't look like it," said the boy, looking around. After so long on the

Harriet, the first thing he noted was the vastness of it all. He had seen from sea level that the ship was big, of course. In some ways its scale had been even more impressive from that perspective, but now not only did he see the size but also the space. It was eerie and set the boy's nerves jangling, but at the same time it felt tremendously good to stretch his legs again at last.

They went down some steps from the raised foredeck, back along the main deck and then up again, up two sets of steps, to the highest deck at the back of the ship. They came to a door. The bear tapped on it with a delicate knuckle and then, after a moment's silence, with a heavy one. There was no reply.

"Let's get in there then," said the boy.

"We can't just barge in," said the bear.

"A captain's cabin is . . ." But the boy had already pushed back the door and poked his head inside.

"Coo-ee! Hello? Ahoy there!" he said.

There was no one there so he went all the way inside, and the bear, muttering darkly, followed him. It was an impressive room, full of finery: intricate ancient charts on a solid-looking desk; behind the desk, an ornately carved chair with a fine patterned silk cover on its cushioned seat; a painting of a sea battle in a fancy golden frame on one wood-panelled wall; a shiny brass lantern hanging from the ceiling.

"Ooh, now this is nice," said the bear, gazing around, impressed at the luxurious quarters of a fellow captain.

"Captain's not here," said the boy, tugging him hard by an arm back towards the door. "Where's the kitchen?"

"Oh, the galley'll be below decks somewhere," said the bear, stumbling back out into the light. "Follow me."

They headed back down to the main deck and from there through a hatch and down steep wooden steps into the half-light of the ship's interior, where the boy's

briefly forgotten fear returned. Above decks had been empty of all signs of life; here below there was still no one to be seen, but every sign that there once had been. They were in the crew's sleeping quarters which was crammed with too many rough wooden bunks, each of them still covered with dishevelled blankets. Here and there were items of clothing – a waistcoat, a jacket, a hat – all of a style from centuries ago but looking, from their condition, only a few years old. On the floor were playing cards, set down mid-game next to coins of a kind the boy had never seen before. It was as if life had been going on here only moments ago and then suddenly everyone had just disappeared. The boy shivered. The bear sniffed the air.

"What do you smell now?" said the boy.

"Danger!" said the bear.

The boy looked alarmed. The bear

sniffed again.

"Or maybe marmalade," said the bear.

The boy gave him a dubious stare.

"Possibly both," said the bear. He set off cheerfully towards a door at the far end of the sleeping quarters, the boy pacing after him.

They passed through another set of quarters, as empty of life and full of mystery as the first, through a further door and down some steps into darkness.

"Where are you taking us?" said the boy.

There was a scratching sound and a match flared into life. The bear held it up near his face, illuminating it as he answered the boy.

"Just following my nose," he said, tapping his snout. They were at another door which he now pushed open. Somewhere in the room beyond, the feeble light from the match found shining metal to glint off.

"Ow!" said the bear and the fading flame of the match, burned right down to the bear's paw, dropped to the floor and expired, sending them into a darkness seemingly deeper than ever before.

The bear struck another match and carried its faint halo of light into the room. The boy stumbled part-way in after him, squinting into the gloom, trying to make sense of the shapes that swam almost into focus then sank back into darkness as the bear moved around.

There was a loud clanging sound and the bear came to a halt.

"Ow!" said the bear again. He lifted the burning match and then raised his other paw beside it to steady the lantern that he had just set swinging with his head.

"Aha!" he said and the firefly light of

the match bloomed and expanded inside the lantern, and the room revealed itself to them. The lantern hung above a simple, sturdy wooden table with a large, sharp knife upon it. On one wall hung a variety of brass saucepans. On another there were some shelves containing various tins, bottles and jars. Beneath these were some wooden boxes and small barrels stacked rather precariously on the floor, a number of unmarked brown sacks slumped beside them. The bear looked into one and then, after a shake of his head, another.

"Here we go," he said. "Biscuits!"

"Really?" said the boy. "Are they chocolate ones?"

"Ah, not that kind of biscuit. These are ship's biscuits. Hard tack." He held one out to the boy. The boy took it and examined it closely. It looked pretty much like an ordinary biscuit but one of the boring ones that he would only eat at home when all the interesting ones had gone. And it was thinner than a proper biscuit. But it looked like it might not kill him. He took a bite. It was very hard and dry and tasted almost of nothing at all, only not as nice. It was the boringest food he had ever eaten and it disappeared in two seconds.

"That was horrible," he said. "Are there any more?"

There were. He had another eight, the last three made more palatable by the addition of a surprisingly good marmalade that the bear found in a cupboard full of interesting jars.

"So," said the boy, speaking with his mouth full and spitting crumbs, "it wasn't danger you smelled then."

"Maybe not," said the bear. He looked serious and seemed about to say something else, but then he was distracted by the discovery of some dried meat ("What kind of meat?" asked the boy; "Best not to ask," said the bear), the chewing of which took all their effort and concentration, and rendered any further conversation impossible.

When they had had enough, the bear got his ukulele out of the suitcase and played it and sang some songs. The boy joined in as best he could, but couldn't really get hold of the tune and didn't know the words. Eventually he just sang something else entirely at the same time. The bear seemed not to notice the difference, or perhaps he just didn't care. The boy was enjoying himself too.

In a break between songs the boy said, "So can you sail this thing?"

"Well," said the bear, "with the sails so torn and without a crew it'd be quite tricky but, yes, of course I could."

"Great!" said the boy.

"But I'm not going to, obviously," said the bear. "We'll get back on the *Harriet*."

"But why? Why do we have to be cooped up together on a silly little rowing boat when we could have all this space and marmalade, and you wouldn't have to row?"

The bear gave the boy a stern look.

"The *Harriet* is my boat. I'm the captain. This ship has some other captain. Just because he isn't here right now doesn't mean we can go stealing it. We're not pirates."

The boy thought about arguing, but could see that the bear was decided and determined on this matter.

"We'll take some more of the food though," said the bear. "I'll leave a note telling them what we've, um, borrowed." Then he set about cramming all the food he could – biscuits and bottles and meats and jars – into two of the sacks. He handed the smaller one to the boy and they headed up and out and back towards the *Harriet*. The boy, dragging his sack along the deck, soon fell some way behind the bear who carried his as if it weighed nothing at all. By the time the boy came up the steps from the main deck to the foredeck, the sack clumping up the steps behind him, the bear must have been back at the rope for some time. Something was wrong. The bear was looking over the side of the ship, slumped over the rail as if he had begun to deflate. As the boy got closer he thought he heard a tiny sob.

He stood next to the bear.

"Um, is something the matter?" said the boy.

The bear turned his head a touch, but only looked at the boy out of the corner of his eye. He raised a forlorn arm and made a weak pointing gesture down at the sea. The boy looked over the rail.

"Oh," he said.

He looked back at the bear who seemed to be growing floppier and sadder with each passing moment.

"Um," said the boy.

He looked back over the rail to make sure he had seen what he thought he had seen.

The rope trailed down the side of the ship. On the end of it was the thinner rope that the boy had tied to it. On the end of that was nothing at all. A quick look around revealed only an empty sea in all directions. The *Harriet* was gone.

"Ooh," said the boy.

Still the bear did not look at him.

"You were meant," said the bear, "to tie the other end to the *Harriet*."

"I did. I tied it to the metal thing that the oar goes in."

"What kind of knot did you use?" The bear's voice was heavy, sad and quiet.

"Well, it wasn't exactly a knot. Not precisely. I just sort of . . . wrapped it around a few times." The boy, listening to himself as he spoke, realised that this didn't sound good. "It seemed safe at the time," he said in an apologetic whisper. He thought the bear would be angry, but he didn't say anything or do anything, he just stood there, slumped over the rail, gazing sadly down at where the *Harriet* should have been but wasn't.

"Sorry," said the boy.

The bear took in a very deep breath very slowly and then let it all out again in a long, sad sigh, like a gigantic tyre with a puncture, leaving himself more crumpled and deflated than ever.

"It's not your fault," said the bear at

last, in a voice full of disappointment and defeat. "I should have done it myself."

"Sorry," said the boy again, but the bear didn't reply or move. The boy could think of nothing more to say so he stood there awkwardly, watching him for a while, and then shuffled away. He wished he could make the bear feel just a little better somehow, but the only thing he could think to do didn't seem nearly enough. But it was all he had. He ran back down the steps to the main deck, leaving the bear drably slouched over the rail, still and sad and broken-looking.

Oops

It wasn't a very loud bang but it was enough to rouse the bear. He unfolded himself and stood smartly up, turning to see the boy approaching at some speed carrying the suitcase.

"Did you hear that?" said the bear.

"What?" said the boy.

"That bang."

"Er, no. I don't think so. Look, I was thinking, you're right, it'd be wrong to take this ship. Maybe if there was a lifeboat on board somewhere then we could borrow that and it'd be quite cosy, more like the *Harriet*, and you might feel better about it."

"No, there's nothing. I looked," said the bear. "I'm afraid we'll have to take the ship. I don't like it, but it does look like there's been no one aboard for a long old while so hopefully there'll be no harm done."

"No lifeboats at all?" said the boy.

"No," said the bear. He looked at the boy more closely.

"Why is your face so dirty?" he said.

"Is it?" said the boy.

"Yes. Really black."

"Oh, that's odd," said the boy, licking a

hand and rubbing at his cheek.

"Looks like soot," said the bear.

"Mm?" said the boy.

"Are you sure you didn't hear a bang earlier?"

"Thunder maybe?"

"No, not thunder. I know thunder when I hear it." The bear stared hard at the boy now, assessing the evidence in his dirty face, his fidgeting manner, his restless expression.

"What have you done?"

"Nothing," said the boy, looking anywhere except into the bear's eyes.

"Really?" said the bear.

"Well," said the boy, "I just thought I'd make you some tea."

"Oh," said the bear.

"Because I thought it might cheer you up."

"Mm?"

"So I tried to light your stove."

"Oh dear," said the bear.

"It's a bit tricky that stove, isn't it?" said the boy, adjusting his stance as the deck sloped to one side beneath his feet.

"Yes, it takes a bit of getting used to," said the bear.

Somewhere above them there was a loud kerfuffle of flapping wings which turned into a steady fading flap. Neither of them looked up to watch the bird's departure.

"And did the explosion make a *very* big hole in the ship?" said the bear.

"Quite big, yes," said the boy. "Sorry."

"I wondered why my feet were getting wet," said the bear.

The sea, having very poor table manners, swallowed down *The Mermaid* with rude haste. The hole in the hull that the boy's accident with the stove had made quickly widened as water surged into it, tearing free great chunks of wood. The vessel filled with water and plummeted down. The bear managed to hang on to the suitcase as they abandoned ship, but the sacks of food, heavy to begin with, quickly became saturated, tugged themselves free of the bear's grip and sank down. One half-full jar of marmalade bobbed back up to the surface, but the rest of the food followed *The Mermaid* down into the deep dark depths. The sinking hulk sucked at the sea above it and a downward tide pulled hard at the boy's legs. The bear threw a thick, furry arm around him and held him up as the churning water slapped insolently at their faces. They kicked and flapped and spluttered and eventually the waters calmed around them. They floated, the

boy gasping for breath, the bear sturdy as an island, amid scatterings of barrels, torn planks and ripped sailcloth. Somewhere, high and far away, a bright blue bird said "*Kark!*"

"What do we do now?" said the boy.

"Better swim," said the bear. "You remember the rock on the map?"

"Yes."

"Well, that's not far. We'll go there. It's quite a big rock, I think. Almost a small island. Might be quite nice, you never know."

"And you know where it is?" said the boy.

"Yes," said the bear with confidence. "This way." He raised a paw above the surface and pointed with a small but certain gesture.

"OK," said the boy.

They put the suitcase on a fragment of

The Mermaid's hull that was floating nearby and, holding onto it, kicked their legs and made slow progress in the direction the bear had indicated.

"So it might have trees and food and water and stuff, this island?" said the boy.

"Maybe," said the bear. "I've never been so I can't be sure. It's rather out of the way. I'm not sure anyone's ever been there, actually."

"Oh, right," said the boy. "So if we're the first to go on to it do we get to name it?"

"I'm not sure," said the bear. "Maybe. Yes. Yes, why not?"

"Great!" said the boy. "We can name it after me."

They both thought about this for a moment, though in different ways.

"Unless it's horrible," said the boy. "Then we can name it after you."

240

"Thanks," said the bear.

"You're welcome," said the boy.

They kicked on. They didn't say much more as the boy was soon too exhausted to speak. After a while, the bear suggested the boy should climb on his back and rest a while, so he did. The sun was sinking now and the boy nestled his face into the fur between the bear's shoulder blades. His wet shirt was beginning to dry a little in the still warm sun and there was more heat rising into him from the bear. Despite the desperate situation, the boy felt strangely cosy. He was drowsy now, his eyelids dropping, then springing back open. He focused on the bear's fur, close against his face, each hair sharply defined in the beautiful golden light then blurring again as exhaustion pushed him towards sleep. He could feel the bear's slow, strong heartbeat bumping up against his chest with a comforting steady rhythm. He could hear that the bear was humming a tune. He tried to make it out, but it was too quiet. It could have been anything.

He closed his eyes to concentrate better and the darkness hugged him to sleep.

Dry Land

When the boy awoke the first thing that he saw was the bear's knees. At first he thought they were still on the *Harriet*, but then he recognised that the surface beneath him was stone rather than wood and remembered, with a pang of guilt, that the *Harriet* was lost. But at least the bear had got them to the island, it seemed. He felt stiff as he pushed himself part-way upright, as if the hardness of the rock had somehow seeped into him, and his eyes and head were fuzzy and half asleep.

"Hello, bear," he said, blearily rubbing at his eyes and trying to focus.

"Oh, hello, boy," said the bear. He was sitting on his suitcase with his back to the sea, looking down at the captain's hat in his paws. Now he put it back on his head, blinked, and regarded the boy.

"You really did know the way, then?" said the boy.

"Of course," said the bear. "We were lucky, actually. It wasn't too far and there was an anomaly in the currents that helped us on the way."

"Have you had time to explore much of the place yet?"

"Um, yes."

"How's it look?" said the boy, yawning and stretching.

"Er, see for yourself." The bear waved a paw over the boy's shoulder.

The boy turned his head and saw for himself.

It wasn't an island, it was just a rock. There wasn't a single tree or plant to be seen. It wasn't even a very big rock. It certainly wasn't a pretty one. And it was almost as cluttered as the *Harriet* had been, as various bits of flotsam from *The Mermaid* seemed to have washed up onto it.

"Oh, this is useless. We're on a cold, wet, ugly rock full of junk," said the boy. "We're naming it after you, then."

"The sea's over there if you'd prefer it," said the bear, pointing. "It's roomier, but it's not so dry. Take your pick. Anyway, we're not stopping long."

"Oh, great. Where are we swimming to next?"

"We're not swimming. I'm building a raft."

The boy took another look at the scattered bits of wood and other bits and pieces around the place. There were some reasonably intact planks and some empty barrels. There was also a section of mast with some rigging attached, so they had some rope to work with at least. And there was more such debris floating in the waters around the rock. If they swam out a little they could gather in some more material for the raft. He was about to suggest this to the bear when he noticed how wet his fur was. The bear had been busy while the boy had been asleep. Not much of the wood had drifted onto the rock unaided.

"That's a good idea," said the boy quietly. "Can I help?"

"Yes, said the bear, "but I'm tying all the knots."

They worked quietly but happily together. The boy was hungry and still tired despite his sleep, but he helped where he could. Much of the wood was too heavy for him to carry, but he could roll the barrels along and sometimes he was able to hold things in place while the bear lashed them together. He did as he was told and made himself useful and the raft slowly began to take shape. At lunchtime they stopped and ate the marmalade, the boy working every last scrap of it out of the jar with a finger. Afterwards he was sleepy again.

"Have a nap," said the bear, spotting a yawn that the boy had tried to hide. "I can do this next bit on my own and I'll need you fresh and alert when we set off."

The boy knew that the bear could have done all of it without him, really. He wanted to insist on helping, but from his sitting position it was far easier to lie down, just for a moment, than it was to stand up. So he lay down and found that the cold wet rock was surprisingly warm and soft. He closed his eyes, just for a moment.

When he opened them again the light had changed and the bear was tying a rope to the mast of the raft. It looked like it was finished, more or less.

"That was quick," said the boy.

"Not really," said the bear. "You've been asleep for hours. And snoring."

"I don't snore," said the boy. "Do I?"

"Just a bit. I thought that monster's dad was coming to get us. Had me worried till I realised it was you."

The boy looked hurt, but only a little. He took a closer look at the raft.

"It's a bit wonky-looking, isn't it?" he said, pointing.

"Well, I had to improvise a lot, with such limited materials to work with," said the bear, "so it's no *Harriet*, I grant you, but it's sturdy enough."

"Will it float?"

"Of course it will float," said the bear. He looked at the raft thoughtfully. "I think."

"Well, can't we shove it in the water and find out?" said the boy.

"Not just yet. The tide's gone out. We'll

have to wait for it to come back in."

"Oh," said the boy, and looked away from the raft to the sea.

"Oh!" said the boy again.

The tide had indeed gone out. It had gone out rather a lot. The water level had fallen by a good twenty metres. The island they were on, it turned out, was a tall column of rock, the sides of which dropped straight down to the sea. The boy looked cautiously over the edge to the distant waves, and felt rather dizzy. He stepped back and sat down.

"That's not normal is it?" he said.

"It is a bit unusual," admitted the bear. "It's probably down to—"

"Unforeseeable anomalies in the currents?" said the boy.

"That's right," said the bear. "How did you know that?"

"Lucky guess," said the boy.

"Anyway, we'll just have to wait for the tide to come back in, and then we can set off. In the meantime we need to get the sail on."

The bear had managed to salvage a tablecloth from the debris of *The Mermaid*.

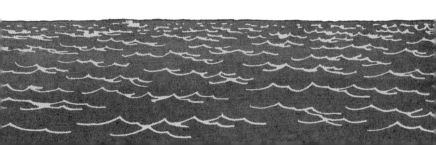

He held it up for the boy to see.

"It's a bit small," said the boy.

"A bit, yes," said the bear. "But it's not such a big raft."

"And there are a lot of holes in it," said the boy.

"Well, if you've got a sewing kit with you then feel free to fix them," said the bear a little testily. "But otherwise it will have to do. It'll be fine, you'll see."

He tied it on to the crossbar at the top of the mast. Then he tied the bottom corners to the base of the raft. He stood back with the boy and looked at the end result.

"Well," said the bear, "it's not pretty, but I reckon it'll go well enough."

The boy could only agree. It really wasn't at all pretty; it was ragged and scruffy and just plain funny-looking. But it was also oddly impressive. It looked strong and safe, as if it would survive weeks at sea with no trouble at all. The boy wasn't entirely sure it would float, but he was certainly confident that it wouldn't fall apart. It was magnificent, in its way.

"Actually," he said, "that's pretty amazing."

The bear didn't say anything. He was about to smile but a sudden gust of wind stopped him.

"Oh!" he said. "We'd better . . ."

But it was too late. The raft's sail billowed up and the raft sailed off the island and dropped out of sight. The boy and the bear ran the short distance to the edge of the rock and gazed down to watch in horror as the raft, after an elegant mid-air somersault, hit the water, rocked briefly from side to side, and then sailed off at considerable speed. It shrank away into the distance. The boy and the bear watched it go.

"Well," said the boy, "you were right about that sail."

A Temporary Promotion

The bear sat on the suitcase and watched the raft until it was a speck on the horizon. Then he watched the speck until it disappeared. Then he watched the horizon. He sat there, silent, staring at the line where the cloudless blue sky met the featureless blue sea. The boy looked at him. The bear was absolutely still, as if frozen or turned to stone. And though he still made no sound and nothing altered in his expression, the boy thought he saw

255

something change in his eyes. It must have been a trick of the light, except the sun was steady and the sky was cloudless, so actually the light had not changed at all. But it seemed as if, somehow, the bear's eyes darkened as the boy watched them. Like the bulb of a torch whose batteries were running down, they dimmed until there was nothing there but depthless shadow. As if inside the bear there was nothing left.

"It could be worse," said the boy.

The bear, his dead eyes still facing out to sea, barely moved his mouth as he replied.

"How?" he said, in a flat, quiet voice.

The boy thought about this for a moment and found that he couldn't come up with a good answer, so he decided to change the subject.

"What do we do now?" said the boy.

This, at least, caused the bear to move, if only a little. He inclined his head towards the boy, eyeing him sadly.

"I don't know."

Then he turned his unseeing stare back out to sea.

"Nothing, I suppose," he said. "Nothing we do does any good anyway so we may as well do nothing."

"That's no way for a captain to talk," said the boy.

"No, you're right," said the bear.

The boy brightened a little.

"But what sort of captain loses his boat?" said the bear. "In fact, three boats. I've lost three boats in one day. That must be some kind of record."

The boy wished he could come up with something reassuring to say but he couldn't help thinking that actually, yes, it probably was a record.

"I must be the worst ship's captain ever," said the bear in a flat voice.

"No," said the boy. "No, you're not. You're a good captain. You've just been a bit . . . unlucky, that's all."

"No. I'm no kind of a captain at all," said the bear, still quietly and with no emotion in his voice, as if he was simply stating a fact about which he had no real feelings.

"Of course you are. You're a brilliant

captain."

"You don't really think that," said the bear.

"Of course I do," said the boy.

"No, you don't." The bear had picked up a piece of paper from the ground at his feet. He showed it to the boy. It had writing and a drawing on it.

"Your bottle washed ashore while you were asleep," said the bear. "Who's Richard Skerritt?"

"Oh," said the boy.

It was the message that the boy had put in the bottle days ago. It said:

"To Richard Skerritt," (Richard Skerritt was in the boy's class at school. The boy didn't like him.)

"I am stuck in a stupid boat with a stupid bear having the worst time ever and probably going to die because the stupid bear has got us lost at sea."

Then there was a drawing of the *Harriet* with a not very flattering picture of the bear in the front and an arrow pointing to the back. At the other end of the arrow it said: "Wish you were here."

Then he had signed his name. Then, after that, he had added: "P.S. Wish that I wasn't."

The boy looked up from the scrap of paper to the bear's face. He wasn't angry, but the boy almost wished he was.

"I didn't mean it," said the boy.

The bear said nothing.

"Well," said the boy, "I did mean it then. But I don't mean it now. I know better now. You're a fantastic captain. Best ever. Now come on, Captain Bear, what are we going to do?"

"Stop asking me that. I'm not the captain any more."

"Yes, you are!"

"What of?" said the bear, in the same emotionless monotone. "I've got no boat. What am I the captain of? This rock?" He gave a small, humourless snort. "Well, at least I suppose even I couldn't sink that."

"It doesn't matter about the boats, you're still the captain," said the boy. He was frustrated and angry and scared, and he was beginning to shout. "Of course you're the captain, you're wearing the captain's hat."

The bear was hunched over now, as if all the tension in him was trying to fold him in two. He leaned towards the boy, the tip of his nose just inches from the boy's face, cold, dark, sad eyes staring into him.

"No," he said, simply and quietly, lifting a forlorn paw to his head. "No, I'm not." He took the hat off and dropped it at his feet. They both looked at it lying there for a second. The boy looked up at the bear. He thought about pleading with him some more, but he could see it would do no good.  The bear had had enough. A whirlpool of panic

and hurt and sadness started up in the
boy's stomach, but he swallowed hard and
tried to ignore it. He wanted very much to
cry. But he didn't.

Well, then, he thought. *Here is where we
are.*

And then the boy picked up the hat and
put it on.

He had to push it quite
far back on his head to
keep it from slipping
down over his eyes, so
it hardly gave him an
air of authority, but he
stood up straight and
tried to keep his voice
from quavering.

"Right, then," he said,
"I suppose I'd better take
charge for a while . . ."

The bear was sure to react to this. He was bound to snatch back the captain's hat and take charge again, the boy just knew it. He was as sure as could be. Any moment now . . .

The bear looked at him and said nothing. And then he didn't even look at him, turning his dead eyes away and staring into space.

Oh! thought the boy. *Now what do I do?*

He had no idea, but he thought it best if he at least looked like he did. He walked decisively over to the bear's suitcase and looked inside it. The telescope was in there so he picked it up and stretched it out. He raised it to his eye and looked out at the horizon. It felt like quite a captainy thing to do so he thought he'd stick with it until he had a better idea.

"Now then, first things first," he said. "Let's assess our situation."

He spun slowly around, scanning the sea in all directions and seeing, as he had at once feared and entirely expected, only sky and sea (except for the brief moment when he found himself accidentally looking at the bear, out of focus and greatly magnified, at which point he almost jumped out of his skin in surprise).

With no better ideas springing to his mind, he decided to look all the way round again. "Best to double check," he said, trying his best to sound confident and in charge. The bear looked as if he hadn't even heard him.

"Here," said the boy, "make yourself useful, will you? If I go up on your shoulders I'll see a little bit further. Come on, lift me up."

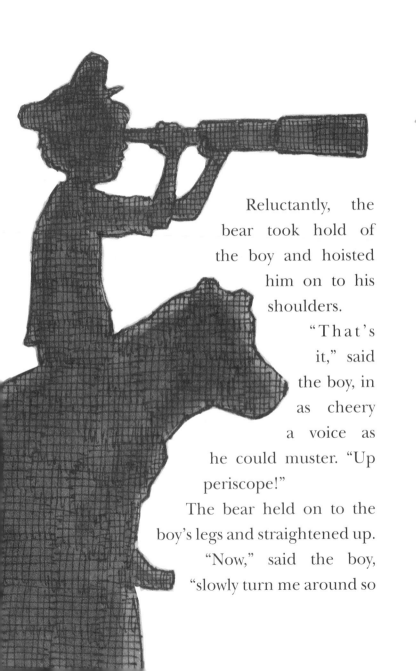

Reluctantly, the bear took hold of the boy and hoisted him on to his shoulders.

"That's it," said the boy, in as cheery a voice as he could muster. "Up periscope!"

The bear held on to the boy's legs and straightened up.

"Now," said the boy, "slowly turn me around so

I can have a proper look at things."

The bear did as he was asked, and shuffled and slowly revolved, turning the boy like some strange living lighthouse. The boy kept the telescope focused on the furthest areas of sea for one turn around, then looked a little closer in for another, then back out, then closer in . . . There was nothing. Even the last of the bits of wreckage from *The Mermaid* were long gone, having drifted away over the horizon in one direction or another. Probably following the raft, like ducklings behind their mother.

"Satisfied?" said the bear. "Will you be getting down now?"

"One more turn around, please," said the boy. "For luck."

"Ha! Luck!" said the bear, but he kept turning.

The boy stared through the telescope so hard that he thought his eyeball must be bulging out. Still he saw nothing, but he couldn't bring himself to say so to the bear. He asked for "one more turn" three more times and the bear, without a word, kept turning. After the third time, he came to a halt.

"There's no point," he said. "There's nothing there, is there?" And his cracking voice broke the boy's heart.

So the boy decided to lie.

"Wait!" he said, though he still saw nothing. "There's something . . ."

His mind was a tangle and he had to try really hard to think at all clearly. *What am I going to do now?* he thought. *I can't make something appear just by wishing it.* But he didn't have any better ideas. *I wish something would appear,* he thought.

"What is it?" said the bear.

Good question, thought the boy. And then he did see. At least, he thought he did. There was the tiniest speck of a bump on the horizon. He had clearly gone mad. He was wanting to see something so badly that he was imagining it. He wiggled the telescope a little to make sure it wasn't just some dust on the lens. He blinked his untrustable eyes hard and looked afresh. It was still there.

"Don't move!" he said to the bear, and his voice was strong and clear, like a captain's. The bear stood very still and the boy felt his arms growing heavy and tired as he held the telescope as still as possible, determined not to lose sight of the tiny fleck of hope.

"I'm not sure yet," he told the bear. "There's something, but it's really close to the horizon and if it's moving at all it's only going slowly. I can't tell yet if it's getting any bigger."

His heavy arms ached and he was cold and tired, but the telescope was absolutely steady in his hands. He watched and he waited and he wished.

"It's coming closer," he said. "I think . . . yes, I'm sure! It's getting bigger. It's coming closer."

And now he could see what it was. He couldn't believe it. He kept the telescope to his eye and blinked and blinked again. It didn't disappear. He wasn't just imagining it.

"It's the *Harriet*!" he said.

A tremble rose up through the bear's shoulders and into the boy and made his view through the telescope wobble.

"She's a long way off, but we might just

be able to swim to her," said the boy. He was speaking quickly now, jabbering excitedly. "Or you could go and I could wait here, maybe."

"We'll both go," said the bear.

"OK," said the boy. "Oh, but we'll have to wait for the tide to come in first . . ."

"It's already in," said the bear, tapping him on the leg.

The boy looked down and saw that the water had risen again, higher this time, entirely submerging the rock. The bear was waist-deep in water, his suitcase floating beside him.

"These tides are really weird," said the boy. "It's not like this at Cromer."

"These are strange waters hereabouts, it's true," said the bear and gently leaned forward, floating up and kicking his legs. "Stay on my shoulders. Now, which way?"

The boy put the telescope back up to his eye and scanned around. Leaning forward over the bear's head, he pointed a definite finger and the bear set off in that direction, pushing the suitcase ahead of him, towards the *Harriet*.

Back On Board

Eager, strong and steady, the bear swam. Fast. He ploughed through the water, his nose just above the surface, his legs churning a white plume. The boy sat up on his shoulders, ecstatic and alive.

They were soon there. The boy stepped up onto the bear's head and climbed into the *Harriet.* The bear dropped in the suitcase and then pulled himself up after it, tipping the boat towards him as he did so. He flopped into the little boat and they sat dripping either side of the centre seat as the boat rocked back to stillness. The bear, though he was soggy and tired, seemed to glow with regained energy. He sat up straight and alert, he smiled and his eyes were full of life again.

The boy grinned, stood up and leaned over to him. He took off the hat and perched it on the bear's head.

"Welcome home, Captain," he said.

The bear said nothing, he just adjusted the hat slightly on his head and sat back on his seat, wiggling his bottom a little as he did so, as if working it into place. Then he took up the oars and began to row.

Splish, splish, splish . . .

The boy climbed onto his seat and sat there thinking. He was back in the stupid little boat with the smelly old bear rowing them who knew where and with no idea when or if they might eat again. And he was utterly content.

"Fancy a game of I Spy?" he said.

"Hmm," said the bear. "Don't mind if I do."

Stormy

S plish, splish, splish . . .

They had played I Spy for a long while. And then, when the boy could stand it no longer, he had gracefully declined another round and reread the comic a couple of times.

He didn't even want to think about when they had last eaten. But his hunger had been there for so long that he'd become used to it. It was normal now and he didn't really notice it.

The bear was humming quietly to himself. He stopped rowing and looked round at where they were heading, off to the horizon, then turned back, looked up at the boy, took off the hat, scratched his head a moment, put the hat back on. Tea breaks and sleeping aside, this was about as long a break from rowing as the boy had ever seen him take. Then the bear squinted, tilted his head to one side, stared off past the boy. Something dark and fearful flickered across his face, a brief glimpse of some worry that he quickly hid away again. The boy had only half noticed it but it was enough to make him ask.

"What's wrong?" he said, turning to look behind him and feeling a sharp blast of wind on his face as he did so.

"I spy with my little eye something beginning with C," said the bear nodding his head to indicate something behind the boat. Surprised, the boy turned his head and stared in the direction the bear had indicated.

The boy could just make out a single small light-grey cloud a long way behind them. He turned back to the bear.

"More inclement weather on the way?" asked the boy cheerily. "Can we row towards it? I could use some rain."

"No," said the bear. "Besides, it'll be on us soon enough."

"Why are you worried about that little thing?" said the boy. "And, in any case, it's miles away." He turned round again to look. The cloud was indeed still a long way away. But it *was* closer now. And bigger. And darker.

The boy watched it, scared and fascinated. He could see it growing, gaining on them and darkening before his eyes. He could hear the tempo of the bear's rowing increase, and the noise of the oars striking the water grow louder and deeper as the bear pulled on them harder, pushing the boat along faster than ever. But the cloud was moving faster still, barging towards them full of menace and violence. Looking back to the bear, he caught another glimpse of worry. His fur bristled in the rising wind.

"Will it be bad?" said the boy.

The bear looked him straight in the eye.

"Yes," he said. "It will be bad."

As he said it, he was thrown into darkness. The boy turned again and saw that the cloud, a brooding black mass, was almost on top of them now.

"OK," said the boy. "What do we do?"

"Hang on, mostly," said the bear. "This

will be an interesting one."

The sea was waking now, stretching and flexing its muscles, then bending, dancing, thumping and bumping and rocking and rolling the boat. The wind came at them hard too, whipping the boy's hair into his eyes, and picking up spray from the sea and throwing it at them. The boy looked up through stinging eyes. The cloud was all he could see of the sky now, looming like a bully, dark and cruel and threatening. And then the rain started. There was no gentle introduction, no gradual progression from dryness to drizzle and then on to rain; instantly, there were hard shafts of water pounding down upon them, pummelling them.

He looked at the bear, already hard to see through the raging downpour. His face was set and his head was in constant motion, looking all around, watching the waves and doing the best he could to keep the *Harriet* level, jabbing at the water with one or other of the oars, steering them through the chaos. He was utterly consumed with the task in hand, and concerned, but not truly afraid. It was clear, even though the boy could only catch glimpses of him through rain and spray and crashing waves, that he was relishing the challenge. He was fighting the sea and he didn't know who would win. The boy wondered if that had ever happened before.

They were ankle-deep in water now, and the boy risked bailing with cupped hands whenever the boat seemed steady enough that he didn't need to hold on tight. The rain bore down onto them one way and the wind tore at them another while the sea, bucking beneath them, tossed them

playfully about.

"This is what you call interesting then, is it?" shouted the boy with as much bravado as he could muster. But he could barely hear himself above the rain and the raging sea and the bear was too consumed by his task to pay him any attention beyond the occasional glance.

The waves were like mountains now and, despite the bear's best efforts to keep the *Harriet* from being buried under them as they crashed down, enough spray had splashed in that the little boat was filling with water. Then the sea picked them up. A gigantic wave rose beneath them, lifting them absurdly high and holding the *Harriet* teetering at its peak. They seemed to hang there for a moment, still and calm, high above the furious waves. Then the tickling foam beneath the *Harriet's* hull tipped them from their perch and sent them plunging down a cliff face of water, crashing into the sea below. The impact threw the boy from his seat, out over the side of the boat. He saw the water, churning and angry, waiting to embrace him, rising to meet him in slow motion. It hadn't occurred to him how calm he had been up until now, up until the moment he became entirely helpless. And even now he was more shocked than terrified. He gasped in the biggest breath he had ever taken and had no expectation of ever taking another.

Then a mighty tug on his arm pulled him back, landing him back in the boat. He looked up, his arm aching, and saw the bear, still fighting the waters with one oar, the other lost to the waves as he had grabbed the boy. The bear gave the boy the briefest, smallest smile. The boy smiled back. Then the *Harriet* span suddenly around and the remaining oar, dug deep into the water, was wrenched from the bear's paw. It flew free and the handle smacked the bear hard on the head. For a fraction of a second he merely looked surprised, then his eyes closed and his body crumpled as consciousness deserted him. The boy leaped up, reaching out to him, grabbing hold of one limp paw. Then the immense wave they had just dropped down began to break above them. The boy stared up at it defiantly, held on hard to the bear and braced himself. He took his next breath. And then the tower of water folded and crumbled and crashed down onto the *Harriet* in a mighty rush of noise and fury, and everything went black.

Calm

The bear awoke.

This, in itself, was something of a surprise. His head hurt, but that seemed like a reasonable trade-off for not being dead. He was lying on his back and the sun was in his eyes. He blinked and squinted, and a hazy shadow took shape before him.

"Hello, Bear," said the boy, who was sitting on his stomach holding the ukulele.

"My ukulele," said the bear, rather groggily.

"You're the boat, this is the paddle," said the boy, holding it up. "Hope you don't mind."

The bear turned his head and realised that he was floating on his back in the sea (an agreeably calm sea) with something hard and buoyant holding his head up.

"I managed to hold on to your suitcase," said the boy. "The storm started to die down after you got knocked out and I used it to keep you afloat."

"That can't have been easy," said the bear.

"I managed," said the boy.

The bear was still looking out to his side rather than at the boy. There was wreckage in the water around them.

"*Harriet*," he said.

"I'm sorry," said the boy.

The bear looked up at him again now. A sadness seeped into his face, softened and then ebbed away. The boy watched it come and go, much as he had expected.

"Can't be helped," said the bear. "Thank you for keeping me afloat."

"You're welcome," said the boy.

The End

Splish, splish, splish . . .

It's quite a stretch for the boy, perched on the bear's belly, to reach down to the water with the ukulele to row. It dips only part-way in, and every so often he has to empty out the water that accumulates inside it. They are making slow progress.

"You know, if you played the banjo we'd be going much faster now," says the boy.

"Sorry about that," says the bear.

"That's OK," says the boy.

"Do you know where we're going?" says the bear.

"Yes," says the boy.

Splish, splish, splish . . .

"You could kick your feet a bit, you know, if you wanted to help out."

"Oh, yes," says the bear. "OK."

The bear kicks his feet a bit and they move on, rising and falling together over the gentle swell of the water.

"Now we're getting somewhere," says the boy.

"Jolly good," says the bear. And, after a pause, "Do you think we're nearly there yet?"

The boy looks ahead and away to where the sun is sinking into the sea.

"Yes, Bear," he says. "I'm sure we are."

And the boy paddles and the bear kicks his feet and, after a while, they sing a little.

And they disappear over that flat blue horizon and on towards another.